W9-CHM-016

JAN 1998

LOVE
FOR
SALE

LOVE
FOR
SALE

A Gideon Lowry Mystery

JOHN
LESLIE

POCKET BOOKS

New York   London   Toronto   Sydney   Tokyo   Singapore

POCKET BOOKS, a division of Simon & Schuster Inc.
1230 Avenue of the Americas, New York, NY 10020

Leslie, John, 1944–
    Love for sale : a Gideon Lowry mystery / John Leslie.
        p.   cm.
    ISBN 0-671-51127-0
    1. Private investigators—Florida—Key West—Fiction.
2. Pianists—Florida—Key West—Fiction. 3. Key West (Fla.)—
Fiction. I. Title.
PS3562.E8174L6   1997
813'.54—dc20   96-8554
                                                              CIP

First Pocket Books hardcover printing January 1997

10 9 8 7 6 5 4 3 2 1

For B.E.

LOVE

FOR

SALE

It was a day to die for. The still air held the tenderest of
lovers' sighs and the morning light was hard as diamonds
as it bounced off the tropical foliage, sparkling against the
waxy, variegated croton leaves and playing over the sim-
mering flowers of the big, bright-hued hibiscus.

Not that I was consciously thinking of dying as I made
my way through the early morning to meet the judge. He
had called the night before asking me to breakfast at the
drugstore where I often ate.

It was unlike the judge to call and want to break bread
on a Friday morning, a workday, so I had, I suppose, a
certain sense of foreboding. The judge was Just Watson,
Key West's circuit judge for more than thirty years and a
distant cousin of my late father's by marriage.

As a young man, Just had returned to Key West from
law school in Gainesville soon after the end of the war,
before I was even in high school. I remember nothing
remarkable about him from that time, just another easy-

going, sociable guy who joined an established Key West law firm, married, and would probably have lived out his life without any further distinction had it not been for the tragedy that occurred a few years later when his young wife, several months pregnant with their first child, was killed in a car accident, forced off the road by a drunken driver one afternoon while she was driving up the old Overseas Highway to visit friends on another key.

Just went into a decline, withdrawing from society, and was seldom seen, outside of occasional court appearances, for more than a year. When he eventually resumed his life, he was changed. Remote, older, older than his peers, he became unapproachable except for legal matters and his passion for fishing. Just devoted his life to law, becoming something of a recognized legal scholar in Florida, and within ten years, before he was thirty-five, he was elected a justice of the peace.

When the circuit judges replaced the old JP system, he was elected repeatedly, forsaking any other advances within the judicial system. Just never remarried—some said he was wedded to the law and would have to be carried from the courthouse to the cemetery, that he would never retire. Of course that was mere wishful thinking on the part of Key West's citizenry, such was the high esteem in which they held the judge.

My mother, Phyllis, had given him the nickname Just many years ago, honoring his integrity, and the name had stuck to the point that I doubted there was anyone in town any longer who could even recall his given name.

I crossed Duval Street on my way to the drugstore, admiring as I passed the rosy bougainvillea growing in untamed abundance along a fence. I found Just seated alone at a corner table with a cup of coffee and the morning paper in front of him.

Even though it was Friday, he was in his civilian attire.

In place of the lawyer's suit and tie, he had on a pair of chinos and a plaid cotton shirt, the sleeves rolled midway up his forearms. Just shifted the paper to the empty chair beside him when I came up, saying, "Bud, sit, sit."

I took a seat opposite him. A faint aroma of cigar smoke seemed part of his natural odor after so many years of faithfully smoking Romeo & Juliet panatelas, although I'd heard he had recently given them up.

"How do you, Bud?"

"I'm fine. How about you?"

Unlike me, Just was not a habitué of this place. He was a loner, seldom seen in any public places where his fellow conchs congregated, in order, I suspected, to avoid being accosted by them about some trifling legal matter. Despite his popular reputation, Just traveled alone; he worked and fished—in that order, and when he sought out company, as he did mine from time to time, there was more often than not a purpose to it other than a mere social encounter. I looked him over to see if I could detect anything. He seemed tense, a quality I did not associate with the judge, who was normally laid-back.

"I'm going to retire," he said.

A waitress brought my coffee and took our breakfast orders.

I was stunned by this announcement. Like everyone else who knew him, I would have guessed that Judge Watson would have been on the bench until he felt he could no longer perform his judicial duties. I studied him to see if I could detect signs of illness. His hair was mostly white, but there was still plenty of it, and for a man approaching seventy he seemed fit.

The judge was tall, thin, his face seldom betraying emotion. It was as if after his wife's tragic accident he had made some conscious decision never to express outwardly any sign of pain; or perhaps nothing could hurt

3

him again in the way that he had once been hurt. His deep-set, hooded eyes carried a sad, somewhat haunted look, but beyond that, his expression was enigmatic.

"You okay?" I asked.

Just waved a hand in front of him as if to ward off any suggestion of frailty. The waitress put our breakfasts in front of us. "Never better." And as if to prove it, he tucked into his eggs, grits, and link sausages with the gusto of a teenager. For a while we ate in silence.

"You still playing the clubs?"

"Off and on," I said. "Whenever there's work." Besides operating a detective agency on Duval Street, I played piano occasionally in one nightclub or another. Lately, I'd been having a hard time making a living in either the detective or the music business.

"I might have a gig for you."

"You?" I was genuinely surprised. I could not remember seeing Just's face even once in any nightclub where I'd ever played. I didn't associate him with the pleasures attendant on sitting in a darkened bar with a piano for company. "What kind of a gig?"

Just took a bite of Cuban toast. "A little reception I'm planning."

"For your retirement?"

"Not exactly." He chewed the toast and washed it down with coffee. "A wedding reception."

"Who's getting married?"

"I am."

The judge. It was more than a title, it was an identity. You heard an old-timer refer to the judge and there was no doubt whom he referred to—always Just Watson. I didn't know anyone who didn't respect the judge. He believed that politics had no place on the bench, and whatever decisions he rendered from his position there, they were always in strict adherence to the law, without regard to politics or personalities.

I was now beginning to see that the respect he summoned was in no small measure due to the distance he kept from those who might come to stand before him in court. Which was any one of us; which meant that he had few, if any, close personal friendships. Who had gotten to know him over the years? Apart from a few distant cousins scattered around this small island, I had always thought of myself as belonging to whatever inner circle, or family, the judge had when he wanted company.

We had played poker on occasion late into the night with tumblers of rum in a cloud of cigar smoke; we had fished together from his flats skiff; and although I had sought his counsel more than once on some case I'd been involved in, I now realized that it was usually me, my dilemmas that were discussed, not the judge's. One didn't intrude into his personal domain.

Her name was Ardis Whelan, Just said, over refills of coffee. She had a house in Key West where she'd spent several weeks each winter for the past twelve years. Three years ago when her husband died, she had begun spending most of the winter here. She was twelve years younger than Just and had a nineteen-year-old son, who was a bit of a problem.

My first thought was perhaps uncharitable: She's an outsider, what does she want with Just? It was the nature of my people to be suspicious of the motives of outsiders. Even though my mother had been an outsider, as were two of my three wives, it was hard to dispel the suspicion inbred in island people.

"She's got money," Just said, as though reading my mind. "Her husband left her secure."

I nodded. I knew nothing of the judge's financial situation except that he seemed comfortable. "Isn't it a little sudden?"

Just shook his head. "I've known Ardis for a few years. We began seeing each other last winter."

With his penchant for privacy I wasn't really surprised that he could have been conducting an affair without public awareness. I smiled. "Congratulations."

"We'd like you to come to dinner tomorrow night. I want you to meet Ardis. Can you make it?"

"Sure. Look forward to it."

Just added some sugar to a fresh pour of coffee and stirred for several seconds. He seemed on the verge of saying something else, then thought better of it. We chatted for a few more minutes, during which time I sensed a certain anxiety emanating from him, but I didn't ask about it. If he wanted to talk, he would talk; he wasn't going to divulge anything until he was ready. I'd been around him long enough to know that.

We finished our coffee. Just reached for the check. I let him pay, then wandered back home with a nagging sense of trouble.

◇

Although my office on upper Duval Street was several blocks distant from the congested downtown traffic, the twin windows on either side of the door advertising LOWRY INVESTIGATIVE SERVICES were clouded with dust. I let myself in the front door, into a large room with scuffed hardwood floors, a desk, and a couple of ancient green metal filling cabinets against one wall. Two overhead paddle fans whirred slowly, sifting the humid air. A wicker chair sat in front of the desk, its emptiness a depressing reminder of the lack of clients.

I closed the venetian blinds on the windows, then walked down the narrow hallway to the back where a modest kitchen was next to my bedroom and bath. Home. I went into the bathroom and peed before returning to the office. Framed photos of my mother and father and brother, Carl, all dead now, hung on the wall behind my desk. I straightened them, as I did routinely, while the pendulum clock kept its indifferent vigil over my activities.

1

The light on the answering machine was blinking. Punching the message button, I listened to the familiar voice of Casey calling from Miami, where she had been living for at least a year. I had seen her only once since she'd left here—last summer when she'd returned with a new boyfriend.

Casey had helped me get sober, and despite an on-again, off-again relationship, I always knew that neither Key West nor I would be able to hold her. I was too old; Key West was too small. Casey had taken her talents as a graphic artist to Miami. I was surprised to hear from her, less surprised when I called back and she gave me her news.

"I'm getting married, Bud." She sounded happy, unlike Just, whose happiness had seemed tinged with anxiety.

"Must be something in the air."

"What?"

"Sorry, congratulations."

"Is everything okay?"

I recognized Casey's code expression, questioning whether I was drinking again. "I'm fine. You're the second person this morning to tell me about marriage plans."

"Oh." I thought I detected some disappointment in her voice.

"It's okay. I just wondered if it's catching."

She laughed then, the easy, natural laugh that brought back memories. I pushed them aside. "Do I know the lucky guy?"

"I brought him down last summer, you remember?"

Vaguely. Nice enough, I remembered, but perhaps not good enough. Then again, there wouldn't be anyone good enough for Casey, I knew. Including me.

"What does he do?" I sound like her father, I thought.

"He has his own advertising company."

"So he's solvent at least?"

Casey laughed. "He does very well."

"You work for him?"

"No. Oh, occasionally some freelance stuff, but I think it's better to keep that part of our lives separate."

"Family?"

"What about it?"

"You going to have one?"

Again the laugh. "Don't you think I'm a little old for that?"

"Forty-something, that's not so old today."

"Well, it isn't an issue, and if we do decide to, we'll adopt."

Yes, of course. Like me, Casey was an alcoholic. Unlike me, she hadn't had a drink in fifteen years or more, but I knew that she considered alcoholism genetic. She would not be predisposed to subject a child to the battle she'd gone through herself.

"Who else?" Casey asked.

"Who else what?"

"Is getting married."

"The judge. I just came from having breakfast with him."

"No!"

"Yes." Casey knew the judge, had heard me talk about him often enough.

"What a coincidence."

"What? The two of you getting married?"

"Not only. I heard something about him the other day and I thought of calling you then."

"We're practically off the map down here. What are you going to hear about the judge in Miami?"

"You'd be surprised. Mike has got some Key West accounts."

9

"Mike?"

"My fiancé."

Oh, yes, him.

"One of his accounts is with the powerboat races there. It's very lucrative."

I could imagine. They came in once a year, corporate-sponsored pilots trailering the huge Cigarette boats, some of them worth a half million dollars, little more than floating fuel containers attached to several high-performance engines. Beyond noise and speed, I had never understood their spectator appeal.

"What's the connection?"

"A guy by the name of Brendan Scott races one of the boats. He's also in the treasure-salvaging business down there. His right-hand man, Delgado, lives in Key West. You ever heard of them, Bud?"

I tried to think. I would have recognized a local name. I couldn't place either one, I told Casey.

"Well, they apparently have some legal wrangles and Just Watson's name was mentioned. That's all I know, but I thought of you when I heard it."

I couldn't imagine that would have been the source of the judge's anxiety when I met with him, but I wrote both Delgado's and Scott's name down anyway.

"I'm inviting you to the wedding, Bud. I'll send a more formal invitation, but I wanted to call you first. Will you come?"

Miami, only a hundred and fifty miles from here, seemed far away.

"When is it?"

"Next month. May tenth." Casey laughed. "I know you don't like leaving that island, but it would mean a lot to me."

And probably to me, I thought, but weddings and funerals were two ceremonies I could do without, having starred in three of the former and attended far too many of the latter recently. To me, weddings and funerals always seemed somehow linked.

"If it means so much to you, I'll try to get up there," I said, perhaps with too little enthusiasm.

"Thanks, Bud. I think of you as family, you know."

Yes, I knew. Despite her newfound success, I knew that we both clung to the same slender thread that was our strength, and perhaps our burden.

After hanging up, I felt the onset of desire, a need for sex, brought on no doubt by Casey's lusty laugh and the distinct if somewhat faded memories of our past couplings. I no longer frequented bars, other than the one I occasionally performed in, and at my age, the women I knew were mostly either married or involved. Seduction had become a task filled with peril. I pulled out a tattered copy of the phone book from the top desk drawer and looked in the yellow pages under *E* for escort services. There were two. I was familiar with one of them. I picked up the phone and called the number listed, listening as a recording came from the answering machine. I recognized the voice, soft, enticing. I thought about hanging up, then spoke my name and number and was about to hang up with the phone was picked up at the other end. "Gideon?" It was the same enticing voice as the recorded message. "What a surprise hearing from you after such a long time. Where have you been hiding?"

From the bottom right drawer of the desk where he slept, the tomcat who lived with me lifted his head, looked up at me, wiped a paw across his face, then went back to sleep.

"Right here," I said. "Just don't get around much anymore, Val."

The voice tinkled with laughter. "I hope that's going to change."

"It is, at least for an evening. I'm looking for a dinner date."

Val twittered. "You've come to the right place. Give me the particulars and let me see what I can do for you."

3

◇

Moonlight and roses. The moonlight was reflected, drifting across the water, illuminating a wedge of calm, darkened sea just beyond the windows. The roses were in a slender vase in the center of the table. Across the same table was a slender brunette, smiling, rather pretty really, with slightly crooked teeth and a teasing quality of her smile. She wore a sheath dress, tight and brightly colored. She wasn't Casey, but Katy Morgan stirred the blood. Val had done just fine.

Katy had developed certain skills. Conversation wasn't awkward. She had a thousand questions, many of them I preferred to sidestep. But by dessert I realized she knew far more about me than I did about her. She was also drinking. I wasn't, but I took pleasure in every sip of wine she took.

"Let's talk about you," I said.

"Me?" Katy shrugged. She wasn't much past thirty, but her manner was somewhat world-weary, as if she'd seen it all, and then some. "I'm not interesting."

"I've seen you around town. I didn't know you worked for Val."

Katy shrugged. "Off and on. I have to take a lot of time off. The burnout rate's high."

"So's the risk, I would think."

"I've got ways of dealing with that." She licked some chocolate mousse from her upper lip.

My blood flowed south, downhill, then up, defying gravity. I could have pursued the moment, but decided to wait, delay, heightening the intensity. "Anything else you would rather be doing?"

Katy smiled, nodded, glancing downward at the table. "Sometimes I think I'd like to go back to school."

"And study what?"

She looked up. "I don't know. Maybe physical therapy. It pays good."

I smiled. She was teasing.

"Do you think that's funny?" She wasn't teasing.

"Not at all. But why PT?"

Katy reflected. "Partly the money, I guess. But I think I'd like working with people. People with problems."

Like me, I thought.

Then she shook her head. "Then other times I think it's silly. It takes a long time and school's expensive and I'm not a very good student. Maybe it's just a dumb dream. What do you think?" She took another bite of mousse.

"If you're really interested in it, why not give it a try. You haven't got anything to lose."

Katy smiled. "You're a conch, aren't you? I can tell by your accent."

"I am. Born and raised here, something generation. I don't remember how many."

"You conchs are like that. Always qualifying. Third generation. Fourth. Does it make any difference?"

"No. Just a matter of pride, some dogged possessiveness about this island."

"I was born here, too. First generation. But somehow I don't think of myself like that. As a native I mean."

"Why not?"

I liked the way her hair moved when Katy shook her head. "I don't know. I just don't have any real roots to this place."

Sometimes I regretted that my own roots went so deep. "Do you want anything else?" I didn't eat dessert, but I took a vicarious pleasure in watching her eat hers, just as I did watching her drink.

"No. How about you. Do *you* want something else?"

"Yes."

"What?"

"You."

"You know the rules?"

"It's been a while."

"Come on. I'll whisper them to you on the way to your place."

I paid the bill and we quickly found a cab in the parking lot.

Beyond conversation Katy had certain other skills. Her hands were warm and soft and delicately scented, the fragrance of the rose that she had taken from the vase still lingered, somehow clinging to her. On the cab ride home she whispered many things, and not all of them had to do with rules.

At home, in the dark except for moonlight spilling in the bedroom window, Katy's practiced fingers undid buttons, belt, snaps, laces, and clothing—slowly. Miles Davis wailed from a tape in the kitchen.

In the moonlight Katy, naked, a silhouette in front of the window, was nearly perfect: her flesh firm yet supple, her breasts high, the light rosy-colored nipples tipped like twin peaks of meringue, her butt swollen like a question mark. She was something from the past, my youth tauntingly rejoined if only for a moment, an hour. Even the necessity of latex brought back memories. Nevertheless, I savored, knowing I would pay for the rejoinder.

Afterward, Katy lay back on the bed and smoked a cigarette, allowing me a certain intimacy with her body, the lingering residue of passion.

She dumped dead ash into an ashtray resting in the center of her stomach, close to where my face explored. I watched the brightening glow of cinder as she inhaled, her body trembling just so slightly. Miles was dragging out a long D-flat in a minor key. I wanted a drink, the jagged sweet taste of rum, which would have mixed so well with the island taste I already had in my mouth.

Miles finished; Katy finished. The cigarette, like my youth, was spent.

"I don't usually do that," Katy said. "You're nice, Gideon."

Later, we stood in my office, Katy back in the tight sheath dress. Shirtless, wearing khakis, I stood beside her, running my hand through the soft tangle of her hair, slightly damp now, trying to hang on to something before turning on the overhead fan. A musty odor drifted up from our bodies.

"Who's that?" Katy stared at the photos on the wall behind my desk.

"My mother and father. And brother."

"Dead?"

I nodded. A long time now, but they remained a presence, persistent as memory.

"What was he like?"

"My father?"

"Did you like him?"

It was a strange question because Captain Billy had

16

been such an enigma. Like him? I had hated him at times, admired something in him at other times, but I'd spent most of my life trying to understand him, and my relationship to him. In the end, I suppose he would remain an enigma. And I would never be able to satisfactorily explain my feelings about him, a man who had chosen to die by his own hand rather than face certain death from the cancer that had riddled his body.

"He was complicated," I said, shrugging off the question.

Katy suddenly looked sad, as if she were going to cry. "Until just recently I didn't know my father, not even what he looked like. And my mother never talked about him."

"How did you find him?"

She shook her head, looking away. "I didn't. He found me."

Sensing some sudden vulnerability in Katy, I didn't pursue it. We remained in front of the photographs, Katy staring at them as if they could speak. I didn't say anything.

"He walked out on my mother and me when I was a baby," Katy continued. I put my arm around her shoulders and gave her a hug. Katy laughed, but the sound was somehow hollow. "Sometimes finding your father isn't so easy." As she leaned into me, I felt warm moisture from her eyes leak onto my bare chest. "Oh, it's so silly to cry about the past. I didn't want to do this."

"It's okay," I said, not knowing what else to say. I wanted to know why it hadn't been easy for her to have her father suddenly in her life, but some instinct told me not to pry right now.

"I never really thought about it. My mother's dead, too. Now I kind of obsess about it. I guess you do, too."

"Some," I admitted.

Katy straightened up. "Well, I'd better go."

I reached for my wallet and took out a hundred-dollar bill and gave it to her. It was more than I could afford, and I knew it was unlikely I would repeat such an extravagance anytime soon. She tucked the bill in the little evening bag she was carrying while I called a cab. We went out and sat on the porch swing while we waited for her taxi. It was late, almost two o'clock in the morning, and we sat there without talking, the creak of the swing reminding me of the times I'd sat here with Casey.

When the cab pulled up, Katy kissed me on the cheek. "I'll see you around." She stepped lightly off the porch and got in the back of the cab, giving me a little wave good-bye. That reminded me of Casey, too.

4

◇

The next morning I slept late. By eight o'clock the sun was streaming through the bedroom window, the same window where last night the moon had brightened the dreary, familiar setting. I got up, put the coffeepot on, and showered, washing away Katy Morgan's lingering scent.

It was too late for me to go over to the drugstore; by now it would be packed with tourists, so I went next door to the Cuban *grocería*, grabbed a half carton of eggs, a small package of bacon, and the newspaper, and returned home.

I sat at the kitchen table reading and eating, getting up now and then to refill my coffee mug. The back door was open, and despite the concrete wall of the motel that loomed two stories above and fifty feet away from my back porch, a cool breeze somehow managed to drift in and flutter around the kitchen, lifting the fur on the back of the cat while he lay on the hardwood floor near the table. I watched the flicker of Tom's whiskers as he slept.

When I finished, I scraped the remains of my breakfast

into Tom's bowl and did the dishes. It was ten o'clock before I was finally ready to get a grip on the day. Not that there was anything that couldn't wait. I'd decided to wash the front windows that advertised LOWRY INVESTIGATIVE SERVICES, in the idle and probably misguided belief that a clean window would bring business. I got out the bucket and squeegee, filling the bucket with soapy water before carrying it all out to the front porch.

Duval Street was awash in traffic, most of it sunburned kids on mopeds, bleating their horns and playing bumper tag as they squandered the days of spring break. Duval Street had become a commercial sideshow. Along with two or three other holdouts I was one of the last who still maintained a residence there. Everyone else had sold out and moved on, either deeper into the residential area, or out of town altogether. For the most part, my people had given up, uprooted by the burden of taxes or seduced by the lure of money from artificially high property values.

Where I had once lived among friends and neighbors, I was now surrounded by businesses—T-shirt shops, chi-chi boutiques, pricey restaurants and motels. The only places to resist change in this block of Duval were the little Cuban *grocería* next door and me. I seldom even used the front door anymore, avoiding this street that had become more spectacle than thoroughfare.

Almost weekly I was approached by one Realtor or another to put my weathered frame house, now nearly a hundred years old, on the market. I could have sold out and raked in a small fortune. Then sat back and watched it be bulldozed to the ground to make room for some garish cinder-block storefront. No thanks.

There were, of course, other options. I could have leased it and moved back into one of those neighborhoods where the claws of commercialism had yet to reach. Out of spite or stubbornness, I don't know which, I had stayed on, keeping the dusty venetian blinds pulled close against the view of encroaching deterioration, hunkered down like some relic from a lost world.

I thought about the judge, a relic, too, and about Casey, who had fled. I thought about the coincidence of their respective marriages, and soon I was transported back to the night before, reliving the evening with Katy Morgan. Which was where I was when she showed up on the porch. She had on a pair of denim shorts and a white T-shirt with an abstract design painted on the front.

"Borne in on a memory." I grinned.

"What?"

"I was just thinking about you."

"Oh. Can I come in?" She looked younger than she had last night, perhaps because of the way she was dressed but also because she looked as if she had just gotten up. Her face was slightly puffy and red like a child's.

I pushed open the door with my foot and followed her in, carrying my window-washing tools, which I put in the corner.

Katy seemed a little uncertain. She glanced around as if she were sure she should be here.

"I've got some coffee made. Want a cup?"

She smiled. "Sure." She seemed to relax a little.

I went back into the kitchen thinking she would follow me. She didn't. "Take anything in it?" I shouted.

"Sugar. Two."

Carrying two mugs of coffee, I went back into the office. Katy was seated in the chair in front of my desk, so I sat down in the swivel chair behind it.

"This is crazy." She took a sip of coffee. "But I thought you might be able to help me."

"So this isn't a social call, I guess. Too bad."

Katy Morgan made a wry face.

"Sorry," I apologized. "I'd like to help you. What's the problem?"

"I'm afraid." Katy took another hit of coffee. "Well, you'll think I'm crazy."

"I don't think so, Katy. Try me."

She smiled hesitantly, flashing her slightly crooked teeth. "What would you do if you had something that you knew didn't really belong to you but . . ." She hesitated, looking away.

I was used to this. People had a hard time talking about their problems. I wondered if lawyers and doctors had the same problem with their clients and patients. Probably so.

Up until a few years ago most of my work had come from the state attorney's office. I was often called on to produce witnesses to crimes, to take depositions, to track people down. But after a falling out with one of the attorneys in that office, I was seldom called by that agency any longer. That could all change, of course, if and when a new state attorney took over the office and cleaned the stables. But I wasn't expecting that anytime soon. Now, when I worked, more often than not it was this sort of thing—some form of protection; the recovery of a stolen item; or locating a missing person. And frequently, it was a friend who hired me. The pay wasn't great and the work was sporadic. Nevertheless, it was work.

"Why don't you just tell me about it, Katy, then maybe I can advise you. What do you have?" I half-expected to hear that there was a dispute over a pet that she'd found.

"A piece of treasure."

My interest was piqued. "What kind of treasure?"

"Something from one of the treasure ships."

"A coin?" Any number of Spanish coins had come up as part of the treasure from the Old World wrecks that had been salvaged around here recently. I had a doubloon, part of my late brother's estate, said to be worth around a thousand dollars.

Katy shook her head. "It's a chalice."

"A chalice?"

"Yes." Katy sat on the edge of her seat, her elbows on her knees, her face cradled in her hands in a neat little V, giving her an angelic look. "A wine cup."

That sort of stuff had been brought up, too, part of the crew's tableware, much of it probably more of archaeological value than monetary.

"Is it worth anything?"

"Quite a bit, I was told."

I was surprised. Most of the early salvaging of these wrecks was funded by investors who had been talked into taking a gamble that something of value would be recovered, but it had taken years before the first wreck was even found.

"Can you describe it?"

Katy cleared her throat. "Well, it's gold, set with different kinds of stones."

"What kind of stones?"

"Emeralds, mainly. And others, I don't know, I don't really know what all of them are."

Whatever they were, this certainly wasn't crew's tableware! I had seen pictures of some of these items when they were first salvaged. Speculation on their value ran into the hundreds of thousands of dollars. I suppose because of Katy's occupation I had a hard time adjusting to her having something worth that kind of money.

"Do you know what it's worth?"

Katy lifted her hands away from her face and held up two fingers of her right hand and waved them back and forth.

She wasn't signaling two grand, I didn't think, but I shot her a questioning look.

Her voice cracked when she spoke, and she cleared her throat. "Two hundred thousand. Maybe more."

Jesus! "Where'd you get it, Katy?"

She ducked her head. "I would rather not say."

I could think of a few reasons why she would rather not say, but none of them appealed to me, and from the tension reflected in Katy's eyes I guessed they didn't appeal to her either.

"Are you scared, Katy?"

She nodded, yes.

"But not scared enough to give it back to the person who owns it. Why not?"

She hesitated. She looked away. She ran her fingers through her hair once, then again. She looked back at me. I waited.

"It has to do with my father. Remember I told you about him?"

I remembered that she had only recently come to know him and that something about finding him troubled her.

"Anyway," Katy went on, "if you think about it, it's been stolen a lot of times." She tried to smile. We both knew that wasn't an answer.

"Except that the Incas and the Spaniards and a few generations who claimed that cup as it made its way to the present aren't in a position to contest its ownership now, are they?"

Katy fiddled with her hair again.

"Where is the cup now?"

"In my trailer."

"Where's that?"

"The trailer park down on Simonton."

I knew it. A seedy, run-down place not far from here where trailers were jammed together like eggs in flats, many of them in near derelict condition. And at least one of them with an item probably worth more than all the trailers put together.

"Do you think you're in any danger?" I asked.

"I don't know."

"What do you want me to do?"

Katy stared at me. "This is crazy."

Maybe. But I recognized in her tone a plea for help. It wasn't always easy to define the nature of that help.

"Maybe you could keep it for me? Just until this is settled."

I thought about it. I would be compromised if it was stolen property, not a position I favored if the police should be involved. And my having the cup wouldn't protect Katy if she was in any danger. On the other hand, if it made Katy feel any more secure, then what harm could it do until I could get to the bottom of this? And who could refuse her? "I don't know," I said. "Let me think about it."

Even that much seemed to relieve her. "What do you charge?"

"A hundred a day. And expenses. Which usually don't amount to much unless I have to leave town. I mostly get around on a bicycle."

Katy smiled. "I've seen you." She reached in the pocket of her tight shorts and dug out a bill, handing it to me.

"But I'm not doing anything," I protested.

"You will." She smiled. "I know you will."

I didn't say anything.

"There's one other thing."

"What's that?"

"I'd rather no one know about my connection to any of this."

"I'm going to need more information from you. And if I'm going to help you, I'll have to ask questions. That's what I do."

25

A frown creased her face.

I held the bill between two fingers. "Take this back."

She hesitated before shaking her head. "Just let me sleep on it. Come and see me tomorrow."

"At your trailer?"

Katy nodded and stood up. "Number twelve."

I watched her go to the door, pause, then open it. She tried to smile, giving me the wave I remembered from before as she went out.

I unfolded the bill. It looked as if it was the same hundred I'd given her last night.

The judge lived in the house in which he had been born
and raised. The two-story stone house with a wraparound
porch sat on a double lot. Perhaps because of the brick
wall surrounding it, the place had always reminded me of
a fortress. As a kid I had often played here. There was no
swimming pool, but the wide, grassy lot with shrubbery
and spreading ficus trees had been a magical place to
fritter away hot summer afternoons with my cousins and
our friends. The house itself was imposing, but not as
large as it appeared from the outside. The pillared porch
was spacious, but a central atrium, which served as a
breezeway, took away from the size of the rooms—three
small bedrooms and a bath upstairs, a living and dining
area with a study and bath downstairs. The kitchen was
on the porch at the back of the house, but separated from
the main house as was customary in the tropics at one
time.

Both his mother and father had died in this house, and

Just had lived here when he married. Soon after his wife's death, he began to live more and more in the ground-floor rooms, sleeping in the study surrounded by his law books. On the rare occasions I'd been here in the past few years, the upstairs appeared to be unused. The walls were white but clearly hadn't been painted in ages; the paint was yellowing and peeling in places. The furnishings, too, were mostly white, and old, some pieces having been around as long as I could remember. A slightly musty smell of old cigar smoke pervaded the rooms.

At seven-thirty that evening, I parked the Buick out front and walked through the gate in the brick wall and up the flagstone walk. Lights were on throughout the place, even upstairs. The judge came to the screen door when I knocked. He winked conspiratorially as I came in. "You may find things a little different from the last time you were here," he said.

Considerably different. The walls had been freshly painted in subdued colors, and vases of fresh flowers were everywhere. The furniture was new, and the entire place smelled sweetly of a mix of herbs and spices and a delicate floral scent. As I followed Just into the living room, a woman dressed in a crinkly white pantsuit came across the parquet floor, smiling brightly, her hand outstretched in greeting.

"Ardis—" Just began.

"Gideon," she interrupted him, "Ardis Whelan." We shook hands; hers was soft and cool. She had thick blond hair, cut short, framing an oval face with almond-shaped eyes and a small, delicately freckled nose. She looked younger than she was. "Just has told me so much about you, Gideon."

"We call him Bud," Just said.

"I know, but if it's all the same, I like the name Gideon."

"That's fine," I said. My first wife, Peggy, had given me

the nickname Bud when we were in high school together, and over the years it had replaced my given name among family and old friends.

"Bud, what can I get you to drink?" Just asked.

"A club soda will do."

Just looked at me. "Since when?"

"It's been a while." I was beginning to lose track of when I'd last had a drink, but I still missed that initial hit of rum, the flavor of the Caribbean.

Ardis led me to a new rattan couch with fluffy cushions while Just made drinks at a wicker bar. "I guess this must have come as quite a surprise for you," Ardis said, "our news."

I confessed it had, having never guessed that the judge would marry again.

He brought our drinks over and I toasted them. Ardis smiled at Just, who sat opposite us. "It isn't as sudden as it seems," she said. "We've known each other for a few years. Did Just tell you?"

"He didn't go into details."

"I knew Ardis would want to get into that," Just said.

"Oh, you're so reluctant to talk about yourself," Ardis replied. "It's one of the things I love about you."

Ardis wasn't reluctant to talk about anything. For the next forty-five minutes she described her life up to the time she and Just had met several years ago. Her husband, Jack Whelan, was an engineer who had worked in the oil business. They had spent a lot of time overseas, living six years in an American compound on the Persian Gulf in Saudi Arabia where their only child, Patrick, had gone to school. Later, they moved to Venezuela for a few years. They had bought a vacation house in Key West, planning to live there once Jack retired, which would have been next year had he not died of a massive heart attack three years ago.

I nodded sympathetically. Ardis gazed off into the distance for a moment. Then she said, "I hear that you play the piano, Gideon."

"On occasion."

"Well, the next time you're playing I'd like to hear you. Will you take me?" Ardis asked Just.

"If it's an appropriate place."

I smiled. The judge didn't frequent nightclubs.

"Don't worry about me, I've been in some dives in my time."

"I wasn't worried about you," Just said, deadpan. "I was thinking of my own reputation."

"Horsefeathers," Ardis said. "How's the dinner coming?"

"I'll check on it." Just finished his drink and walked out to the kitchen.

"He's a wonderful man," Ardis said. "And a wonderful cook. I like decorating, but I was never handy in the kitchen. With Jack we most often ate out. I feel very fortunate with Just." A dreamy look came over her and we sat in silence for a while.

"Jack, of course, liked him, too," Ardis continued, staring down at her hands. "He always wanted me to remarry, Jack did, if anything ever happened to him. We had a good life and I can see living the rest of it happily here in Key West with Just. Once he retires, I'd like to get him out of here occasionally and show him the rest of the world."

"I guess you know all about his life."

"Oh, yes, he's told me everything. Such a tragedy. I can't make that up to him, but I think I can make him happy."

"Just mentioned your son."

"Patrick. Yes, Patrick's difficult right now, but I'm hopeful he will grow out of it. He's in between schools and has been working up North. He's going to spend the summer here."

"Has he met Just?"

"Not yet. The problem with Patrick is that he was never close to his father, and I think he feels some responsibility for me, even though he won't admit it." Ardis smiled sadly. She had a mutable face, youthfully ebullient one minute, a concerned, aging mother's the next.

"Dinner's ready," the judge said, coming in from the kitchen.

"Just is teaching me to cook," Ardis said, standing up and smoothing her clothing with a downward motion of her hands. She joined Just, taking his arm.

I followed them into the dining room.

"Don't you think we should tell Gideon about our plans?" Ardis said. Something about her, either nervousness or an excess of energy, kept her in constant motion. Even when she was seated, Ardis's hands fluttered—gesturing, smoothing her clothing, or touching Just's arm as she talked. But what was disconcerting was that she never held anyone's gaze for long; either she looked aloft, or her eyes darted from one thing to another.

Just wiped his mouth with his napkin and took a sip of wine. We sat on leather sling chairs around a wooden table worn dark with age. The judge had baked a whole hogfish and served it with yellow rice and black beans and a plate of fried plantains ripe and sweet.

"I thought you might have explained all that," Just said.

"There were so many other things to talk about I didn't get to it."

Just smiled in my direction. He seemed amused and genuinely happy. I smiled at his good fortune. But Ardis could certainly talk.

"Well, we're getting married Wednesday," Just said. "Patrick will come down on Tuesday. We're going to have a private affair with a notary and family only. You're invited, of course."

"Then on Thursday," Ardis cut in, "we want to have a reception. Just has rented a hall and we'd like for you to play, Gideon. Can you do that?"

"Of course."

"On Friday we're flying down to Cartagena for our honeymoon," Just said.

"In Colombia," Ardis added. "Staying in the old colonial city. I think Just will like it."

"Where will you live?"

"In Cartagena? There's a hotel—"

"In Key West," I said.

Ardis smiled. As a younger woman she must have been beautiful. She still had a good figure, slender, long waisted, with full breasts. Her face was animated, lively, but gravity had begun to take its toll along her jawline and neck.

"Right here," Ardis said.

"Ardis is going to sell her place," Just remarked, looking at her.

"If I can persuade Patrick . . ." For once she left a sentence unfinished.

"He'll come around," Just said, more out of conversation, it seemed, than conviction.

For a moment we ate in silence, then Ardis, apparently not to be restrained, said, "How do you like what we've done here, Gideon?"

"Very homey," I said, thinking of my own spartan bachelor quarters. "Domestic. You've tamed the judge."

"Oh, nonsense. I don't believe he was ever wild. It's fun seeing this place come alive. I'd love to have some parties here."

"Let's take it easy," Just said. "I'm an old man."

"Oh, for heaven's sake, you're not even seventy and look at you. You could pass for fifty."

"Until I start partying."

Ardis put her fork down and touched Just's hand for a moment. Her eyes glistened. "Oh, Justice, we are going to have some fun."

Just smiled awkwardly and drank more wine. I reflected that it had been my mother who had given Just his first nickname all those years ago, and now here was another woman embellishing it. For all of his embarrassment, Just really did seem happy.

We finished eating while Ardis schemed and plotted the future, making up guest lists for future parties, bringing up names of Key West's social elite. Then, as if sensing that Just and I might want to talk together for a moment, she poured him more wine before clearing the table and leaving us alone.

"She's quite a woman," I said. "A lot of energy."

Just shook his head, staring at the glass that he twisted in his large hands. "You know, in some ways she reminds me of Willa. Sort of how I imagine she would have been if she'd lived."

I was in my early teens when Just married his first wife, and though I barely knew her and had only a faint memory of what she looked like, I suppose there was some distant resemblance to Ardis. I was happy for Just now, happy that he had, in some ways, arrived full circle from that point when life seemed to have shut down for him.

"You seemed a little edgy the other day at breakfast," I said. "Not getting cold feet, are you?"

Just studied his wineglass. "A little maybe." He smiled. "From what Ardis tells me, her son's not making it any easier."

"He'll get used to the idea." I spoke with more authority than I felt, never having had children of my own. It sounded right though.

The judge shrugged. "He's still a kid. You remember when you were young?"

"Sure."

"As I recall, you were kind of wild."

I grinned. "Now and then. Still am on occasion." I thought of the evening with Katy.

"So I don't have to tell you of all people, Bud, that sometimes there are things in a man's past that are indelibly stamped."

Of course not. The past was like a birthmark, there as a constant reminder. "Something plaguing you?"

"A little indiscretion," Just said, lowering his voice. I didn't respond, waiting.

"Bud, I haven't had a serious relationship with a woman since Willa." It was a statement of fact rather than a lament. He slid a glance across the room as if to see who might be listening. "I am, however, human."

Human. Of course. To be human was to be frail, and I knew about frailty. Some time ago I had taken what I hoped would be my last drink. There had been demon nights, nights when I sweated out nearly four decades of abusive drinking. Something I had chosen to do, and do alone. I could not bear the thought of going public, of attending meetings, of the constant narcissistic self-analysis that was the proscribed course for most people who wanted to get sober. I didn't knock anyone who took that course, but for me it was a matter of style. And stubborn pride. And throughout that time there had hardly been a day that I didn't want a drink.

So I knew about frailty, although I had never thought of the judge in those terms. I held back a smile. The judge had suddenly become all too human. He seemed now to withdraw. "Bud, this is strictly between us."

I pulled an imaginary zipper across my lips. Just hadn't
taken his eyes off me. He had always reminded me of the
lawyer Gregory Peck had played in *To Kill a Mockingbird*.
Intense, self-effacing.

"Who is she?"

"*She,*" Just said, "is dead. Her daughter lives here
though. Her name is Katy Morgan."

I had a sinking feeling in the pit of my stomach. It must
have registered in my face. "You okay, Bud?"

"You're not going to tell me you're her father, are
you?"

Just shook his head. "Katy thought I was. She came to
me a few months back. Her mother had told her about us
before she died. It was a brief affair, but I guess it mattered
to her. To tell you the truth, she was pregnant at the time
so there was never any question then about me being
the father. She left town soon after her baby was born.
I never thought about it again until Katy got in touch
with me."

"She wanted information about her father?"

Just nodded. "I couldn't help her."

"You know what she does for a living?"

He nodded again. "It put me in an awkward position."

"With Ardis?"

"I didn't tell Ardis about it. But I wasn't sure how
persistent Katy was going to be. You can see how embar-
rassing it could be."

"I don't think you've got anything to worry about."

"You know Katy?"

"We met recently."

Just stared at me with dawning recognition, a thin smile
crossing his face. "What do you mean I don't have anything to worry about?"

"Katy's found her father."

"Whose father?" Silently, Ardis had come in from the kitchen.

Just turned, looking at her uneasily. I stood up. "A case I'm working on," I said. "It's been resolved."

"You lead such an exciting life, Gideon."

"On rare occasions. Most of the time I live like the rest of us, in a world of speculation."

6

◇

I wasn't tired and I didn't feel like going home, so I headed downtown. Duval Street was packed with family-style tourists—mom, dad, the kids, and grandma; all wearing T-shirts with cutesy slogans. They weren't dropping tons of money for the Chamber of Commerce either. Instead, they roamed the streets looking slightly lost and bewildered. Gawkers. I rode the elevator up to the night-club in the hotel where I often played weekend gigs. My friend Ronnie was still tending bar.

It wasn't ten o'clock, still time to pull in a late-night crowd, but the grand piano sat silent while the CD spit out some blues.

"Well, well, speak of stray dogs," Ronnie said when I took a seat at the end of the bar. She had bounced around jobs in the bar scene in Key West for the past few years, somehow managing to survive beyond what I would have considered was a normal shelf life in this occupation. The fact that she was blond, pretty, and sassy probably hadn't hurt her longevity any.

"Tell me something I want to hear," I said.

Ronnie showed her beautiful teeth in a million-dollar smile guaranteed to bring a tip if not one more for the road. "Pepper was just in here. He was talking about getting you to play Friday, through the Easter weekend."

"That's what I want to hear," I said. Pepper was Roger Culpepper, the manager, and he had a particular fondness for the music I played, mostly Gershwin and Cole Porter tunes, which had a limited appeal among the tourist types the promoters were currently encouraging to visit us down here at the end of the road.

"Get you something?" Ronnie asked.

"I suppose I can choke down another club soda. I'm beginning to know what it's like to drown."

Ronnie flashed another smile, served up a glass of the bubbling liquid, and moved off to tend to the more exotic drinkers. I sipped my drink, staring out the darkened glass window that was now like a mirror along the length of the bar. Just's news set me to thinking. I thought about wives and marriage and what had escaped me.

Peggy Baker and I were married in 1956, the summer I returned to Key West after two years in Korea with the U.S. Marine Corps. We had known each other all our lives, playing together as kids in grade school, hanging with each other throughout adolescence, fumbling through our first sexual experiences together. Marriage was a natural extension, and if one could be said to have been made in heaven, ours should have been; but it was not.

Korea had left its mark on me, and when two years later my father took his life, another scar was added, a wound recently reopened when my brother killed himself. For years I had attempted to bury the past in alcohol. And for a time it had worked, but at a price. Among other things, it had cost me my first marriage. The irony, of course, was that Peggy, with all her nurturing instincts, had been prepared to do battle on my behalf with the ghosts from my past. But she could not suffer my drinking, coupled with my refusal to have children.

The marriage lasted a decade, through the better half of the turbulent sixties, before it grounded on the reef of booze and infidelity. I could not, and did not, blame Peggy. And not surprisingly, with so much history between us, we have remained friends.

On the many times over the next couple of decades when we had coffee together, usually in her kitchen, I had had plenty of time to reflect on what was given up, and lost. On balance, I'd long ago decided that we were both better off. Peggy had gone on to marry Jake Maloney, a steady, temperate man with regular hours as an executive with the aqueduct authority, the people who brought us our water a hundred and fifty miles through a pipeline from the mainland, and the father of Peggy's two children, a son now grown, and Barbara, who had graduated last year from Key West High School.

I thought about Just. And Katy Morgan. Since Katy had asked me to keep our relationship discreet, I had refrained from telling him that I was working for her. Just was unduly concerned, I thought, that some tidbit of gossip was going to embarrass him.

The judge was a very private man. I was certain that he had nothing to worry about. Katy had no reason to reveal anything about his relationship with her mother; discretion was the better part of her profession, just as it was of mine. I suspected that it wasn't Ardis's reaction that concerned him so much, but rather that of her son, Patrick.

"Another, Gideon?" Ronnie was back, pulling me from my reverie.

"No, that'll do. Better go home while I can still float."

I turned to get up and noticed a familiar face at the other end of the room. I didn't recognize the man she was with, but the familiar face belonged to Katy Morgan. I sat back down. "On second thought . . . ," I said to Ronnie.

She refilled my glass. I felt an unexpected pang, not so much of jealousy, which would have been silly given Katy's profession, but of longing. Longing that was certainly touched by regret for the certain loss of Casey, but also by a feeling of desire and—more surprisingly—a true sense of fondness for Katy. She meant more to me, I had to admit, than a one-night stand. Seeing her here like this caught me off guard. Then, I remembered she had hired me. I was working for her, so it was only right that I keep an eye on her. I relaxed a little.

"You know the couple in the back there?" I asked Ronnie. A waiter had gone over to take their order.

Ronnie leaned across the bar to get a better look, pushing her long blond hair away from her face as she did. "She comes in often enough, usually with different guys. The way she dresses, I'd say she was a hooker."

Katy was dressed a little more casually than she had been the night we went out. She had on slacks and a white blouse with a linen jacket, sedate enough except that the slacks were just a shade too tight, the blouse open a few inches too low. "She works for an escort service," I said.

"Lucky her. I'll bet she's making a living."

"Saving for a college education."

Ronnie grinned. "From the school of hard knocks."

"What about the guy?"

"I've seen him around, but I don't know him."

The waiter came over and gave Ronnie their order. She moved off to pour a couple of drinks in large balloon glasses. She set them on a tray and the waiter carried them away.

"Mind if I caress the keys? I could use some practice. With no work I've been getting rusty of late."

"Be my guest." Ronnie turned off the CD that was playing as I stepped onto the darkened platform and sat down at the keyboard. I struck a couple of chords, then flowed into a soft, melancholy rendition of "Love for Sale." Katy never looked up, never took her eyes off the guy she was with, her hand resting lightly on his arm.

I watched them, caught up in a sense of nostalgia, remembering similarly intimate evenings with Casey, who bore no resemblance to Katy but for the mood of the moment. Katy had a presence about her, a sadness, maybe, that I couldn't fathom but that nevertheless gripped my imagination. I tried to shift gears by changing keys and songs, wrestling with "Straighten Up and Fly Right," and focusing my attention on Katy's date.

He was youthful but, as far as I could tell, not young, and, like Katy, casually dressed. There was an occasional flash of jewelry when he gestured, some rings on his fingers, a gold chain, maybe even bells on his toes, which were sockless in leather deck shoes.

They drank and whispered, their faces close together. Katy did not seem at all flirtatious. They were more like friends, I thought, than lovers. Or perhaps that was just the way I wanted it. Nevertheless I kept the music soft and romantic, lightly fingering the phrases that lovers had succumbed to for years. Mood music, the kind of stuff so many of us had grown up with.

A few more people came in the bar, adding another layer of noise. I watched as Katy's friend signaled for another round of drinks.

At some point their mood changed. Katy and the guy were arguing. It wasn't loud, or particularly obvious, but I'd been watching them for close to an hour, and now there was a definite difference in their connection. The gestures were no longer slow and easy but sharp and staccato. Katy would talk and the guy would look away—then the other way around. Their expressions were fiery.

Finally, Katy stood up and strode away from the table, heading toward the piano, on her way to the ladies' room, I presumed. As she passed me, I changed keys suddenly, striking a couple of discordant notes, louder than usual, then whipping into "Mack, the Knife." She glanced my way, paused, looked again. Her eyes seemed to have sunk back deep into her skull, so I couldn't be sure she even saw me, or anything else. She was looking inward.

When she came out of the ladies' room, I'd finished playing and stood up from the piano, starting back to the bar, timing it so that our paths would cross.

"Oh, it's *you*," Katy said blankly. She didn't seem pleased or displeased to see me. She still carried a look of woeful sadness.

"Is everything all right?"

"Not tonight it isn't."

"Lovers' quarrel?"

Katy glared at me.

I resisted the impulse to reach out and put my arms around her. I tried to smile. "You hired me to watch out for you, remember?"

Maybe she had just drunk too much. I didn't know her well enough to tell. I had the sense of being in the presence of someone who had just received some terrible news, something so crushing she was unable to respond.

"Katy, can I help?"

She stared down at the floor, shaking her head. "I'm going home. I'm tired."

"When do I see you again?"

She seemed not even to think about it, despondent, lost in whatever distressful news she had just received.

"Noon," she said. But I wasn't sure she knew what she was saying.

Katy ambled over to the table like a sleepwalker, lost in some world of her own. The guy she was with stood up and they went out together. Or rather with each other, but certainly not together. I waited five minutes, then left, too. Very much alone and without any arguments from anyone.

◇

*S*unday bloomed as bright as a yellow hibiscus, nearly a clone of the previous day; without a breeze, the palm fronds hung limp and motionless, the light filtering through their green from a perfectly blue, cloudless sky.

I took the newspapers down to a secluded patch of sand where few tourists ventured and secured them with a rock while I swam for a mile, then came back, toweled down, and sat propped against a lone palm tree to read.

An hour or so later, the tranquillity was shattered by a brigade of adolescents on Jet Skis, screaming and plowing through the thin water in tight circles, rooster tails of spray shooting up behind their plastic toys. I went home, showered, put on a pair of clean khakis and a T-shirt, and went out to breakfast, where I dawdled over coffee and more newsprint.

It was nearly noon when I returned home, noticed the insistent blink of the red light on the answering machine, and punched the button that allowed me to listen to Katy

Morgan's distant, distracted voice. She probably had a hangover, but her tone was almost apologetic as she suggested that I come by at three now instead of noon as she had told me last night, and if she wasn't there to come in and wait for her. The door would be unlocked. Something was strange about it, the tone of voice odd, disjointed, as if whatever had gotten to her last night had not been relieved today. And she was going to leave the door unlocked. Strange. "I got rid of that object we talked about." Pause. "But I still may need your help." There was another longer pause, dead time on the machine, when I had a sense that Katy had not broken the connection, but was debating saying something more. After several seconds came the bleep signaling the end, and I stood staring down at the answering machine while the tape rewound.

I had been looking forward to working for Katy. Not so much for the money but because, I had to admit to myself, it would have been an excuse to see more of her. Now something in her voice left me troubled.

I sat down behind the desk, picked up the phone, and dialed her number. I let it ring a dozen times but there was no answer.

I felt disappointment, probably unreasonable, but given the moody message and her condition last night when I saw her in the club, I wanted to know what was wrong, and I wanted to help her. I wondered if any of this had anything to do with the guy I'd seen her with last night. Or maybe it was my own feelings and I was just blowing things out of proportion. But I wanted to see her again, look in her eyes, and see if I could find my way back over the barrier that she seemed to have put up around herself. Now I was going to have to wait for a couple of hours.

Something wasn't right but I wasn't in a position to say what. And there wasn't much I could do no matter what it was. After sitting around fretting, I finally decided to hell with it and got on my bike and rode over to pay a call on Peggy, my ex-wife.

"Bud, is it my imagination or are you not stopping by as often as you used to?" Peggy asked as I sat down at the Formica-topped kitchen table, a bowl of plastic fruit on a crocheted doily set dead center.

"Like I told the judge the other day, I don't get around much anymore. Where's Jake?"

"Out fishing. That's what he does on the weekends."

Peggy put a mug of coffee in front of me and got the sugar bowl from a cupboard. "Is it true what I hear?" She was a big woman, at one time voluptuous, now heavy-legged with varicose veins, but she still had a pretty face that had been spared the ravages of age. It was as if her body had somehow absorbed all the shock.

"What do you hear?"

"Just is getting married?" Peggy sat down at the table, supporting her chin with a clenched fist.

I nodded. "So it seems."

"Have you met her?"

"I had dinner with them last night."

"What's she like?"

"An organizer, and very social. She's redoing the house and she's making a lot of plans. She wants to travel."

"Do you like her?"

"Well, *I* wouldn't marry her—"

"Oh, Bud, you wouldn't marry anyone."

'She's okay. She talks a lot. But the judge seems happy and he's the one who has to live with her."

"What's her name?"

"Ardis Whelan."

"Not from around here?"

"Nope. Just says she reminds him of Willa."

Peggy stood up, shaking her head. "When are they getting married?" She carried the coffeepot over and refilled my mug.

"Wednesday. There's a reception on Thursday, and Friday they're off to South America for a honeymoon."

Peggy leaned against the counter, folding her arms across her ample chest. "I'm so happy for him. I just hope he knows what he's doing."

"I guess he does, and if he doesn't . . ." I didn't finish the thought. "How are the kids doing now that they're away from home?"

"It's like a new life," Peggy said, a little wistfully, I thought. "I talk to them once in a while on the phone, more frequently to Barbara, but from here on out it's just Jake and me. It's an adjustment."

I nodded.

"What about you, Bud? You don't seem to change at all."

"Nope. Wouldn't know where to begin." I finished my coffee and stood up. Fifteen or twenty minutes here once a month or so was enough somehow to reaffirm my status.

"Do you ever see Webb?"

Webb Conners. At one time my best friend. I hadn't seen him in several months, I told Peggy.

"You should look him up. Judy's worried about him."

Webb and Judy had married soon after Peggy and I had. We had gone to school together and were all close friends at one time. "What's the problem?"

"She says Webb is going through some changes, she isn't sure what it's about."

"She must have some idea. Judy isn't the type to shy away from an opinion."

"Well, for one thing she's worried about his health."

Webb had put on a lot of weight in the past few years. "Has he seen a doctor?"

"It's more than that. Their marriage is affected."

"You mean their sex life? Listen, Peggy, Webb and I aren't as close as we used to be. We don't talk about that sort of thing."

"I know that, but he doesn't have a male friend who's as close as you two once were. You're still probably the one person who could get Webb to talk."

"I doubt it."

"Would you try?"

I stood up, ready to leave. "Sure," I said, more to get away than from any commitment I felt. "It's good to see you, Peggy. Say hello to Jake for me."

On the way home, I stopped at the grocery store and picked up some items. When I got back, no messages were on the answering machine. I put the stuff away and saw it was almost three o'clock. I decided to call before going over. I sat down at the desk and dialed Katy Morgan's number. No answer. For nearly an hour I kept calling, but there was still no answer.

Shortly after four I got on my bike and rode over to the trailer park on Simonton. It was only a few blocks from me, a run-down place that had been in Key West for years. Shaded by several large mahogany trees, many of the trailers never got any direct sunlight, which left their exteriors rusted and moldy. They were crammed in side by side, most of the units fixed and immobile, some with screened-in areas that had apparently been erected by their owners in an attempt to give the basic rectangle of metal and plastic a feeling of homeyness rather than that of dwelling in a tin can.

Rusted gas lines snaked from under the trailers to cylinders of propane; kids' plastic toys, broken and twisted, littered the area, while mangy dogs slept in the shade. As I rode around the dirt square looking for number twelve, I head the howls and screams of kids and the occasional frustrated responses of a female trying to coax some peace.

Number twelve was an ancient Airstream on cinder blocks, the numeral 2 dangling upside down beside the 1 on a rusty mailbox. I chained my bike to a weathered and wobbly two-by-four that supported a makeshift porch railing for the cinder-block steps that led up to the door. I knocked, waited, and knocked again. I couldn't hear any movement inside. It was late afternoon, Sunday, when folks were either at the beach or watching a ball game on TV. I could hear some distant play-by-play coverage coming from open windows. But no one was in sight. There was the smell of food being fried in grease. And the unmistakable odor of gas.

I put my hand on the knob and tested the door. It was unlocked. I opened it a crack and was overwhelmed by the escaping rush of gas from inside the trailer. I flung the door open wide, stepped away for a second, filling my lungs with fresh air before I rushed inside the trailer. "Katy?"

There was no answer because Katy was on the linoleum floor of the small kitchen just to the right of the door, the gaping maw of the oven spewing forth its poison. I stepped over her body, clad in a skimpy satin robe, and turned the oven off before picking her up and carrying her outside.

Under a tree away from the door of the trailer was a small, irregular patch of grass, and I put her down there. Placing two fingers below her neck, I searched unsuccessfully for a pulse. Then I leaned over her, cupped her mouth with my hands, and tried to breathe life into her with slow, even breaths, counting as I breathed, aware of the cool dryness of her lips against mine and the lingering noxious scent of gas.

A woman's voice behind me said, "My God, what's happened? I smelled gas and—"

"Call an ambulance," I said, then continued to try to kiss life into Katy.

I was dimly aware of a crowd that gathered, and in the distance the wail of a siren. When the medics arrived, I stood up, watching as they attached a respirator to Katy. I went back into the trailer and began opening windows and turning on fans.

The trailer seemed even smaller on the inside as I stood in the little kitchen area, a narrow countertop dividing it from the living area. A phone hung on the wall above the counter. The furnishings were old and showed wear, but everything was clean and orderly. A couple of mugs with cartoon characters painted on them were in the sink.

An old teddy bear, propped in the corner of the Scotch-plaid settee in the living room, was staring at me. The coffee table held a miniature TV, some paperback books, and magazines. A chair matching the settee was backed up against the kitchen counter. A couple of lamps and a combination radio and cassette deck on the floor rounded out the living area. Some towels had been placed around the window cracks in a modest effort to seal the trailer.

It was a mean place to die.

I followed the short, narrow hallway to the back of the trailer. A bathroom I could barely turn around in had a shower and a small sink and toilet. The vanity above the sink was stocked with cosmetics. I backed out into the hall.

Opposite the bathroom was a closed door to the only other room in the trailer. I opened it and stepped inside Katy's tiny bedroom. I could practically feel the despair that was etched into the thin, scarred fiberboard on the walls of her bedroom; at the base of the wall, a panel had come loose, exposing its cardboardlike interior.

Briefly I looked around the room, in the closet at the foot of the bed, in the single drawer of a bedside table. I got on my knees and looked under the bed. I didn't find any treasure. I didn't find anything except dust and the personal accumulation of a lifetime. A short lifetime.

When I was done, I stepped out onto the wobbly porch to breathe in the moist air and feel the rising heat. The medics had taken the respirator off and covered Katy's lifeless body with a blanket.

Mixed with the fading odor of gas now was the smell of decay all around, and the sense that I was surrounded by desolate angels.

8

◇

One of the two detectives who showed up at the trailer was Bill Eberhardt. His partner, Myles Archer, was a thin, nervous man I'd never met before, but Eberhardt had been on the force for many years. We'd crossed paths often enough over those years for me to form a favorable opinion of him.

Bill was a big guy with a head of silver hair, a ruddy face that was pretty much expressionless. He carried a notepad and pen and wore the kind of wash-and-wear short-sleeve shirt, with tie pulled askew from the neck, that I always associated with him. His eyes, a shade of blue so light they were almost gray, burrowed into whomever he was talking to. Right now that was me.

We stood outside the trailer in the dust stirred up by the crowd, which had grown, and the departure of the ambulance carrying Katy's body. I related what I'd found inside while Bill took notes. I didn't tell them Katy had hired me. We'd get to that soon enough, but I wanted

some time to think about my response. Myles looked
around the trailer, then held the door open for Eberhardt
to go in. I remained outside.

In less than fifteen minutes they were back out.

"Was she a hooker?"

Bill and I wandered over to a far corner of the trailer
park where there was some shade. "She worked for an
escort service," I said.

Those blue eyes bore in. "What do you know about her,
Gideon?"

"I knew her socially." They would get that information
from Val.

Bill jotted something in his notepad. "Anything else?"

"Anything else what?"

"Anything else you want to tell me about her?"

I looked down at my dusty shoes. "I don't know much."

"But if you remember anything, you'll be in touch,
won't you?"

"Absolutely." I started to turn away.

"By the way, I take it you were here on a social visit."

"That's right. We had an appointment. She told me the
door would be open and to go in if she wasn't here."

Bill stared at me. I stared back. I didn't think there was
anything in it, just a kind of acknowledgment. "Suicide?"

"That's the way it looks," I said.

"Was she depressed?"

"She was definitely upset. The last I heard from her
was a message on my answering machine this morning.
She sounded distracted. She didn't say anything about it
though. That was one of the reasons I came over. To talk
to her."

"What were the other reasons?"

I shrugged. I needed time to think. I still had the taste of
Katy's lips on my mouth, the smell of gas in my nostrils. I
felt pain and anger. If I had gotten over here earlier—who

knows how much earlier?—maybe fifteen minutes, maybe an hour, I was sure I could have saved her. I should have come when I got that message, heard the despair in her voice, especially since I knew her mood when I saw her last night. But I had no reason to share any of this with Bill Eberhardt. Not yet, anyway.

"I'll probably have some more questions for you, Gideon. Going to be around?"

"Just like always." I thought about hanging around, paying some final respects to Katy, but then said to hell with it. My being here wasn't going to do her any good. I could best do that by finding out what had happened to her. I got on my bike and left. When I got home, I called Val.

"I can't believe it. Katy?" Val sobbed. I heard her blow her nose. "Gideon, this is terrible news."

"I know it is. I liked Katy. There was something about her. Did she have a date this afternoon? Do you have a record of it?"

"Just a minute."

I heard Val put the receiver down and move away from the phone. She came back a moment later stifling tears. "No, I don't have a record of anything for Katy until tomorrow night."

"She say anything about meeting anyone?"

"No, why? I thought you said it was suicide."

"It looks that way, but I have no way of knowing for sure. Did she seem depressed?"

Val seemed to think about it. "The last time I talked to her was on Friday when you called. She seemed fine then."

"Did Katy have a drug problem?"

"Not that I know of."

"Would you have been aware if she'd had one?" The coroner would answer this sooner or later. I wanted it sooner. Especially if she was on downers.

"Probably," Val said, "but Katy was different, you know."

Sure she was, I thought. She was working for Val because it provided the most money in the shortest time for her to achieve her goals. Katy had wanted to get out of Key West, get back to college and become a physical therapist. It wasn't the sort of orientation I would have expected from one of Val's girls.

"She was special," Val added.

I agreed. But I wondered what Val considered special. "What was so special about her?"

"Oh, I can't put it into words. There was a lot to her—you knew it even if she didn't let you get close to her . . ." Val's voice trailed off. "Is this going to cause me problems, Gideon? Are the police going to start looking into my business?"

"I'm sure they'll want to ask you some questions, but you're legit, aren't you?"

"Of course, as long as there aren't too many incidents like this."

"I saw her out with someone Saturday night. Do you know who it was?"

"I can check. Hang on a minute."

I waited as Val skimmed through whatever records she kept.

"This is confidential," Val said. "I'm not supposed to do this."

"Katy's dead. She had an argument with a guy on Saturday night. The police are probably going to want those receipts."

"Gideon, this is just between you and me, all right?"

"Of course."

"His name's Brendan Scott."

"You know him?"

"He's used my services on occasion."

"Local?"

"I don't think so. I think he comes here on business."

"Always asked for Katy?"

"I don't remember."

"You know what Scott does?"

"I think he might be with one of the treasure salvors outfits. A lot of those guys asked for Katy, and some of them were from out of town."

"Thanks, Val. You've been a big help."

"What do I do if the police want my client list?"

"Give it to them. And maybe you'd better make a spare in case I need one."

Val said she would. "Something else about Katy."

"What's that?"

"She was fragile. She tried to cover it, but there was a definite fragility about her. And in this line of business that never hurt anyone."

"Until now."

I hung up. I thought about calling Just, but decided that could wait. Instead, I searched the phone book for Brendan Scott. He was not listed. Then I rifled through the yellow pages in search of phone numbers for the various treasure-salvaging operations that had sprung up around here after Mel Fisher's famous find nearly a decade ago when he salvaged the estimated $400-million cargo from the *Atocha*, a sixteenth-century Spanish brigantine that had gone down in a hurricane a few miles off Key West.

It had taken Fisher fifteen years of quiet desperation before he found what he described as the "mother lode," which spawned a small but competitive industry in the Keys.

Nothing of such magnitude had been salvaged since, though there had been rumors recently that an even larger wreck had been discovered and the race was on to find it.

I called Fisher's office to ask for Brendan Scott. There

was no answer. It was Sunday. I called the treasure museum and the person who answered said no one by that name worked for them. A couple of other salvage companies were listed and I tried them, but no one was there.

Last night was the last time I saw Katy Morgan alive. If it was Scott she had been with, and he was from out of town, it was possible that he was still here. I began calling the upscale hotels and resorts and finally got lucky at the Pier House.

"He's in room three fourteen," a female voice said. "Shall I ring him for you?"

"Please." I listened through six or seven unanswered rings before hanging up, then looked at the clock behind me. It was going on seven o'clock, right around sunset. I put on a pair of cheap dark glasses and rode my bike into the sun to the other end of Duval Street and chained it to a rack outside the Pier House.

At the front desk I was given directions to Brendan Scott's room before setting out on an odyssey that led outside, where I followed a meandering path bordered by thick foliage, around the swimming pool, through a bar, across the sandy beach, from one complex of buildings to another before I found the one that housed 314. It turned out to be a suite. I knocked on the door. No answer.

I prowled the hallway, running my hand over the textured concrete walls. Occasionally someone would pass me on the way in or out of one of the rooms. The sun had set but a rosy glow still emanated from the western sky, which I could see from windows at one end of the hall.

Half an hour or so after I arrived, a man in flip-flops and a white beach robe approached 314.

"Brendan Scott?" I asked.

The man looked up. He was portly, with prominent features made more so by thinning hair and a sunburn. He was not the man I had seen with Katy Morgan.

He looked me over, took in the khaki pants and worn T-shirt, apparently trying to decide if I was anyone he had to acknowledge. "What can I do for you?"

"I wonder if we could talk for a minute."

"About?" He had the key in the lock.

"Katy Morgan."

Scott looked up, expressionless, then pushed the door open. "I don't think so," he said, starting into the room.

"She's dead."

Scott was about to close the door, then hesitated a fraction of a second too long, and I stepped across the threshold. "Wait a minute!"

"You were out with her the other night," I said, cutting him off, aware that I was breaking my vow to Val, but I had no choice.

"What's it to you? You don't look like a cop to me."

"Private."

He seemed to size me up again, then jerked his head in a way that I took to be an invitation inside. I moved into the room while Brendan Scott closed the door.

The suite had a sunken living room and a doorway that led to a bedroom where I could see an unmade bed littered with items of clothing, all of which seemed to be male.

"I had dinner with Katy Morgan Saturday night," Scott said, walking to a bar where he poured himself a tumbler of Scotch and added a couple of ice cubes, which disappeared into the glass with a splash like a cannonball off the low board. He didn't offer me a thing.

"Just dinner?"

"Just dinner." He moved over to a white settee and sat down, tucking the robe around his girth.

"But you'd been out with Katy on other occasions."

"Sometimes, when I was in town."

"How often was that?"

"What is this? Why are you giving me the third degree?" He drank half of his drink in one swallow.

"What it is, is practice for the real thing, once the cops do show up."

"Don't do me any favors."

"I won't. How well did you know Katy?"

He swirled the remaining Scotch in his glass, staring at it. "Not very well. How did she die?"

It was the first interest he had taken in her. "Gas."

He looked up from his drink. "Suicide?"

"No one knows. I found her lying on her kitchen floor, the oven on."

Scott frowned. He seemed to be thinking about something. Maybe the news of Katy's death had touched him in some way. "You found her?"

"That's right. I had an appointment with her."

"In her trailer?" Scott got up and refilled his glass. He had changed, grown remote, though perhaps less antagonistic. Something almost conspiratorial was in his manner.

"I knew Katy. She asked me to come over."

"What for?" he asked, a little too casually.

"What do you care?"

"You're a private. Maybe you were working for her."

"Maybe I was. What's it to you?"

Scott went back to studying his drink some more.

"Did you ask her to come back here with you?"

"What?" He seemed dreamy, almost startled by the question.

"The night you were out with her. Did you ask her to come back here with you?

"No, I was tired. I was in bed by ten-thirty. Alone."

"Where did she go?"

"How would I know? It was none of my business. She got paid for going to dinner with me. That's it."

"Where did you leave her?"

"I dropped her off at a hotel on Duval Street."

"What time?"

"Ten o'clock. Thereabouts."

"Was she drunk?"

"I don't think so. We had a couple of drinks before dinner and shared a bottle of wine."

Perfect. He didn't need practice. I had the feeling I was talking to someone who had been through interrogations before; he knew how to handle them, straight on, no hesitations, just the facts, his facts, as he wanted them presented. Except for a quick, furtive look he shot me over the rim of his glass, he might have been perfectly at ease, just working out some business deal. The cops might go to work on him if they had reason to believe Katy's death was something more than an accident and that Brendan Scott was lying, but I couldn't—not without a scene, and I didn't want a scene right now.

"You're good," I said. "What do you do?"

"Investments. I make them."

I nodded. "I hope the others turn out better than Katy Morgan," I said, and left.

9

◇

The night was born in on a wave, slow moving, rolling, like the wake from a large ship plowing the edge of the Gulf Stream miles from shore. From my office window I watched as the western sky seemed to shudder with the last of the dying light. I felt the weight of the night, and the sudden need for distraction.

My ancient Buick, a '73 Electra that had once been eggshell blue before twenty years of the tropical sun and salt air had faded its color a smoky gray pockmarked with rust, was parked on the side street. It took a few minutes to fire and then trailed blue smoke as I drove into New Town to the Cineplex, where I watched an action-adventure that had been partially filmed in the Keys. A muscle-bound beefcake played the lead role. Apart from the on-location setting, it captured nothing of what life was like here. We had allowed ourselves to be turned into a scenic backdrop, I thought, and this was what we got for it. It wasn't very good—but it was distraction.

Afterward, I returned home, cooked dinner, frying some chicken wings in a hot, zesty oil I'd spiced up with garlic and cayenne pepper, preparing some mashed potatoes from a box, and heating frozen corn. A bachelor dinner designed for efficiency if not taste.

After doing the dishes I went into the bedroom and sat down at the old upright with its soundboard exposed. The middle E-key was stuck and I worked with the action for a while trying to free it, then gave up and played for an hour, going through my repertoire. I really was rusty. The aged fingers were stiffening and my phrasing was off. I welcomed the interruption of the phone.

It was the judge: "I heard about Katy Morgan." The coconut telegraph—that breezy island word-of-mouth form of communication that had delivered so many messages across this town—had finally caught up with him. "The word is, Bud, that you found her body."

"The word is accurate."

"And the cause of death. Is that accurate, too?"

"I don't know, it looks that way. We'll have to wait for the coroner's report."

"You think it's got anything to do with what we talked about the other night?"

"I don't know, Just. Between you, me, and the fence post, Katy had hired me. She had something that didn't belong to her, but she felt she had a claim to it. She was afraid of something, but she died before I could find out what. A few hours earlier and I would have been able to save her. And by the way, the police don't know any of this yet."

"What was the something?"

"Katy asked me not to tell anyone, but now that she's dead, I guess it doesn't much matter. It was a wine chalice part of the loot salvaged from one of the treasure ships."

"Why didn't you tell the police?"

"I can't answer that. Partly because I looked around her trailer when I was there and the chalice wasn't there. I don't know, Just. Something in me wanted more time before I told them. It was just a feeling I had. An instinct."

"Did she identify her father?"

"No, she didn't get around to it. Maybe she wouldn't have. Maybe that has nothing to do with her death. I don't know."

"I hope this isn't going to come back to haunt me, Bud."

"I don't see why it would."

"Things have a way of happening. You know that. I wouldn't want to be connected with this in any way given my present circumstances."

A thought struck me. "Your name's not on Val's escort list, is it?"

Just hesitated. "I hope not."

"I could make a discreet check with Val."

"Would you do that?"

"Consider it done."

We hung up. It was late, but Val worked a late-night business. I knew she would be up. She was.

"Have the police called on you yet?"

"Yes, not too long ago either."

"Did they ask for your records?"

A hesitation, a slight stutter, was in Val's voice. "They were particularly interested in the last thirty-six hours. Katy was off today. Gideon . . ."

"Yes, Val?"

"Your name was on the list." She sounded distressed.

"It's okay. I've already told them I knew Katy professionally."

Val heaved a sigh of relief. "I didn't want to get you in any trouble."

"You didn't. Did they take your client list?"

"No, the only names I gave them were for the time they

asked about. Those names came from credit-card receipts. There was nothing for them to take."

"Val, I've got a favor."

"I know you do."

"I'd like to look at that list."

Val chuckled, but with a little edge of nervousness. "You know, honey, I don't have any list of names. Not officially anyway. I'd be a fool and out of business if I turned something like that over to the police. Unofficially, I've got my own black book and I consider that my insurance, you know what I'm saying?"

"I know. I'd just like to take a look at it. Unofficially. Your secrets are safe. I'm trying to get a lead on why Katy died. If this was suicide, the cops aren't going to go too far with it. I'll try not to cause anyone any embarrassment."

"I know I can trust you, Gideon."

Katy had said the same thing and look where it got her. "How about if I come by tomorrow?"

"Sure, but not too early, please."

It was after midnight when I got to bed, and even though I was tired, I couldn't sleep. The moonlight turned my bedroom into a ghost room. I was haunted by Katy's recent visit, stung more than it was easy to admit by her sudden death. She was nearly half my age and it was ridiculous to think that she would have been anything more to me than a casual friend, but even that provoked in me a sadness over her loss.

I picked up a paper volume of the *Four Quartets of T. S. Eliot,* pondering with Eliot present time through time past and the future, while listening to the echoing fall of footsteps in my memory. It was a fractured night.

10

◇

The next morning I was down at the waterfront fuel docks early, the time of day when I was most likely to catch Matt Johnson sober. Most small towns in America, especially waterfront towns, have a guy like Matt Johnson—a colorful old character who has outlived his time and place but, like a ghost, still haunts the lost locales of his youth.

Key West's Matt Johnson had spent most of his life on the sea, until age, booze, and the changing tide of the town made it impossible for him to make a living. Now he spent his time at the docks, hustling tourists for beer money. He'd become a caricature, but, when sober, Matt was still a font of information.

He was sitting on a scarred wooden bench at the end of the rickety dock, watching a muscular, college-age fellow fill the fuel tanks of an expensive sport-fishing boat.

Scraggly gray hair hung down to Matt's shoulders, and tattoos covered his arms. At one time he had worked as a diver in the sponging industry, and later he had shrimped.

He was a master diver and for a while he had hired out on the treasure-salvaging boats, until the drink finally caught up with him and no one would carry him any longer.

"What say, Bud?" Matt glanced up at me but kept an eye on the boat where the guy was filling the tanks. The stomach-turning smell of diesel fumes drifted our way.

"Tell me something, Matt."

"Sure thing, Bud. Can you spare a six-pack?"

I went into the office and came back with a cold six-pack of Rolling Rock. I pulled one of the bottles from the carton and tossed it to Matt, who unscrewed the top and took a short pull, pausing to lick his lips and stare at the bottle before guzzling down half its contents. I held on to the carton.

"Hits the spot, Bud." Matt belched. "What do you need?"

"The name Brendan Scott mean anything to you?"

"Oh, boy, Bud, you hit the jackpot. Last regular paycheck came with his John Hancock on it. What you interested in him for?" He finished his beer and looked toward the carton. I didn't make a move to fish out another bottle.

"What does he do?"

"Shit, Bud, look over there." Matt motioned with his empty bottle to another dock off to his right where an old, rusted ship was tied.

"That's the *Mariposa*. Belongs to Scott?"

"Yep, got a fair amount of my sweat on it, too."

"Treasure hunter?"

Matt nodded. "Surprised you don't know of him. He's been in and out of here for years."

"What's he like?"

"Scott? Hell, I don't know. Only laid eyes on the man a few times. He's got other people running the operation."

"Who would that be?"

"Feller by the name of Delgado. Joe Delgado."

That name rang a bell. "Tell me about him."

"Well, what the hell's there to tell, Bud? He puts his pants on the same way the rest of us do, one leg at a time."

"Any scandals?"

Matt laughed while dividing his attention between the boat in front of us and the six-pack in my hand. "I could sure use another one of those."

I took another bottle out and handed it to him, cradling the rest of the carton under my arm. Matt uncapped the bottle and drank, more slowly now.

"Scandal? Hell, yes, there's scandal. Delgado's always in trouble with the law."

"What kind of trouble?"

"I hear there's a lawsuit over salvage rights to something big. Scott and Delgado are claiming the find."

Now I remembered where I had heard Delgado's name. Casey had mentioned him when she'd called the other day. "Delgado also races boats, doesn't he?"

Johnson got a dreamy look in his eyes. "See, Bud, I knew you'd know these people. Yeah, Delgado's a racerman."

I started to ask him something else when a heavyset guy wearing shorts and a Patagonia shirt came out of the office as the fueling on the boat was completed. Matt Johnson jumped up to greet him.

"Cap, you goin' after the big ones today?"

The big guy swept a look over Johnson and grinned. "I'd planned on it."

"I can lead you right to 'em."

The big guy laughed. "No doubt you could, but we're working our way over to the Bahamas. We won't be back in here for several days."

Matt shifted around on the dock, his body twitching nervously. "You spare a man a beer?"

The big guy looked at me, then back to Matt. "Don't see

why not." He pulled a crumpled bill from his pocket and handed it to Matt, who saluted him. "You're my man."

The big guy eased gingerly down onto the boat and cranked over the engines. Matt came back and sat down, pressing the bill out on his leg. It was a five.

"Yes, sir," Matt said, "the day startin' out mighty fine, Bud. You must be carryin' some luck. You're not goin' to hold that load forever, are you?"

I dropped the six-pack on the bench beside Matt.

"Kind of you, Bud. You got any more questions, you know where to find me."

"Hang in there."

"Hangin'."

I left him and walked back up the dock and across a parking lot to another dock where the salvage boat was berthed. There was no sign of life on board. I hung around for a while before going into a nearby screened-in restaurant where I could sit and keep an eye on the salvage vessel. Twenty minutes went by and I was dawdling over a second cup of coffee, thinking about leaving, when two guys approached the boat. One of them was Brendan Scott. He was having a heated conversation with the other man, whose back was to me, a trim, dark-headed fellow in jeans, T-shirt, and deck shoes. Something about his body posture, his movement, seemed familiar.

I sipped coffee and watched the two of them from a distance of approximately twenty yards. Between the noise in the restaurant and outside, I couldn't hear them. Scott was doing most of the talking, and from his appearance, I judged that he wasn't happy. Occasionally, the other guy would lift his arms as if to make a protest, but to no avail. Scott kept up a steady stream of invective.

After ten minutes or so they turned and approached the gangplank of the salvage vessel. As they walked aboard, I got a better look at the dark-headed guy before they both disappeared into the bowels of the ship. I couldn't be absolutely sure, but I would have been willing to bet that the guy with Scott was Joe Delgado. And Delgado was the same man I'd seen with Katy Morgan Saturday night in the club.

I hung around for another ten minutes and finished my coffee, but no one got on or off the boat. I wandered outside and waited some more. I'd already talked to Scott without much success. And as much as I wanted to talk to Delgado, I preferred to do it when he was alone. After a half hour of standing out in the sun and watching tourists, I decided to go home.

◇

I was on the phone making an appointment to see Val when Ardis Whelan came in the front door. She stood just inside the doorway, one hand on her hip, and looked around, smiling benignly as I cradled the phone. "It's exactly what I would have expected," Ardis said.

"Can I get you something?"

"No, thanks." She sat down in the wicker chair in front of my desk. Her eyes looked troubled, the features of her face tense. The light scent of her perfume changed the air in the room. "I was downtown doing some shopping and decided to look in on the spur of the moment. I hope it's all right."

"Of course. And I suppose it has to do with Just."

"How did you know?"

"We spoke on the phone. Just sounded low." I did not consider that description a betrayal of the judge since I had no intention of revealing the topic of our discussion, but I was surprised when Ardis said, "Oh, of course he's low. He's depressed." She tried to smile.

"Why?"

"Why?" The smile faded and Ardis looked shocked. "You're a man, you should know. He's getting married. Wouldn't you be depressed?"

Probably, but I wasn't aware that the condition was common to all men, I told her.

"Well, that goes to show how much you know." Ardis laughed. "Just has been living alone all of his life, doing things his way until I came along."

I nodded. The judge was certainly independent, his own man.

"You don't simply fall in love like that"—Ardis snapped her fingers—"without some misgivings."

"Are you getting cold feet?"

"Me? Heavens no. But I'll let you in on a secret if you promise not to say anything to Just."

"Well, I—"

"Oh, I know, your damned male bonding and all that. All right, then, it's no secret. I wouldn't have been happy to simply live with him. It's a matter of propriety maybe. He has a reputation, and even though nobody gives a damn anymore, it wouldn't look right at this time in his life to be shacking up with me. And, frankly, I don't want it like that either." She made her speech matter-of-factly, without sign of emotion. Then I sat staring at her while she looked off in the distance, unable or unwilling to meet my eyes.

Finally, I smiled. "Kind of challenging, isn't it?"

Ardis shook her head. "There's nothing challenging about it. But it will pass."

"The depression?"

Ardis smiled, too, now. "Of course that's temporary.

Once all the hoopla's over." She waved her hands in a dismissive gesture.

"Something's bothering you. What is it?"

Ardis straightened her shoulders. "I thought that Just might have confided in you."

"In me?" I studied her face looking for some clue as to what she was thinking, but her features shifted too much for me to read. She did sit forward on the chair expectantly. "I don't think I can help. Besides, your theory sounds pretty good to me."

Ardis shook her head. "I simply want to know if there is anything else troubling him, anything he doesn't feel he can tell me, but which I should know."

I thought of Katy Morgan. "Not that I know of," I lied.

"Has he said anything about my son, Patrick?"

"Well, he's expressed some concern, but I think you already knew about that."

Ardis smoothed her skirt. Her eyes were dark and liquid against her pale skin. "He wasn't unduly stressed?"

"Not unduly. Should he be?"

Ardis shook her head. "I don't think so. Patrick isn't a bad kid."

Something about Ardis Whelan troubled me. She was just a little overly bright and organized with a certain odd skittishness. Maybe she and Just weren't as neatly matched as she tried to make them out to be.

"Anyway," Ardis continued, "Patrick is due to arrive and we're having a party tomorrow night. Will you come?"

"Of course."

"Good." Ardis rose. "Oh, and by the way, I'd rather you didn't mention my visit here to Just. I'm sure everything is going to be okay."

I nodded. Ardis departed, leaving behind the lingering scent of her perfume. I locked the front door behind her and went out the back to the side street and got into the Buick.

Driving on a damaged frame, I crabbed my way up-island to Val's place, a condominium in a high-rise block of concrete that afforded a view of the water but took the sea breeze away from those of us in the hinterland. I thought of the suffocating trailer park where Katy Morgan had lived.

Val opened the door seconds after I rang. I hadn't seen her in a year or more, but she hadn't changed. A vivacious woman, tall, large-boned, heavy-breasted, with a slender waist and delicate complexion, she was wearing a white, smocklike dress that hung down from her shoulders. Her straight blond hair, bleached by the sun, framed an oval face that showed signs of stress. Nevertheless, her habitual smile greeted me.

"Gideon, come in here." Val pulled the door open and ushered me into an incredibly untidy apartment. The furnishings were all modern with much glass and chrome and leather and looked expensive. A large-screen TV was on without the sound. The large room was filled with the sound of New Age mood music meant no doubt to be restful; I found it irritating.

Val kissed me on the cheek, then beckoned toward the sofa. I sank into leather so soft and liquid that I could almost recall my prenatal experience. On the TV screen, goldfish flitted back and forth among coral and seaweed. I stared.

"It's like having an aquarium without the fuss," Val said. "Don't you love it?"

I shook my head, having no idea what to make of it.

"I have it on all day. I find it relaxing." She laughed and sat down on the sofa beside me, curling one bare foot up under her. "Now, how can I help you, Gideon?"

"The name Joe Delgado mean anything to you?"

Val tapped the tip of a manicured finger against her front tooth, her brow furrowed. "I'm not sure. Should I know him?"

"Katy was out with him Saturday night. After she'd had dinner with Brendan Scott."

Val shook her head. "Not on my ticket, she wasn't."

"How does that work?"

"Simple. I set up the dates, charge the clients, who pay me, usually with a credit card, and from that I give the girls a percentage."

"And beyond that?"

"Is their business. I'm in the escort business, not a pimp."

"Kind of a fine line, isn't it?"

Val flashed her wide smile. "Maybe, but it's the line I follow and it keeps my occupational license renewed every year."

"What if one of your girls decides to step out on her own?"

"If I find out about it, she's gone. No questions."

"Was Katy apt to do that?"

"Katy was reliable. I never worried about her. I don't think she would have crossed me."

"So Delgado might have been a boyfriend she met after her date with Scott."

Val stood up. "I don't think Katy had a regular boyfriend. Let me check my records just to make sure." Val disappeared down a hallway and returned a few minutes later with her "black book," which was actually green. She sat back down, thumbing through the pages. "No Delgado."

"Mind if I take a peek?"

Val looked from me to the book. An untypical frown pulled her features together, aging her. "It won't go out of this room, right?"

"I want to find out what happened to Katy. I may have to use what I find in there, but no one but you and me will know where I got it."

Val tapped the book against the palm of one hand. "A deal, right?"

"A deal." We shook hands and Val handed over the book.

I glanced through it. Most of the names meant nothing to me. A few I recognized, some who would have been deeply embarrassed by their revelation. The judge's name was among them. Along with another friend of mine. An old friend. Someone I'd been talking about with my ex-wife Peggy only recently. Webb Conners. I was surprised. I closed the book and handed it back to Val.

"Any others?"

Val shook her head.

"Do you ever amend it?"

"Every so often I go through and clear out old receipts. I keep a list of regular clients and"—Val winked—"any names that might be useful in case there's trouble."

I smiled. The judge's name would certainly have been useful. I stood up. "Thanks, Val, you've been a big help."

Val walked over and surprised me by putting her arms around me. "Gideon, if you're ever in the mood for an evening with an older woman, I can always adjust my schedule."

I smiled, feeling the pleasant softness of her body pressed against mine.

Val laughed. "It was just a thought. By the way, I'm having an annual birthday bash. Why don't you come."

My social life was looking up. Two invitations in one day.

"Sure. I'll be there."

Val gave me the particulars and walked with me to the door. "Just for the record," I said, "did Katy ever mention having picked up a piece of treasure, something of value, from one of her clients?"

Val thought a minute. "No, I don't think so. I'd remember it if she had."

I nodded and left, driving the Buick slowly back home, musing about my old friend Webb Conners.

12

◇

The bell to the front door rang while I was in the kitchen trying to rustle up something for dinner. It was Monday evening, an odd time for a business call, and I wasn't expecting guests. I walked into the office, opened the door, and ushered in the dark-headed man in leather deck shoes, jeans, and T-shirt whom I'd seen a couple of times previously, most recently earlier today at his salvage boat being chewed out by Brendan Scott.

I grinned. "Good to see you. And thanks for dropping in."

Cocking his head, the man blinked a couple of times, a puzzled expression crossing his face. He appeared no more than forty and wore a tan that looked as if it had been permanently pressed there. When he smiled crookedly, his white teeth gleamed against his sun-darkened skin. "You were expecting me?"

"Let's just say I was looking for you. Joe Delgado if I'm not mistaken."

"And you'd be Sherlock Holmes."

"A poor imitation." I motioned to the chair in front of my desk. Sitting down, Delgado propped his right ankle on his left knee.

"Have we met before?"

"Not formally."

"Brendan thought I should look you up."

"That would be Brendan Scott. I wondered if he would send you around here."

Delgado's face maintained a perplexed look. "You seem to be a couple of steps ahead of me. Help me catch up."

"Of course. I talked to Scott yesterday about Katy Morgan. In fact, I believe I was the first person to tell him Katy was dead. This morning I saw him talking to you at the boat. He didn't look all that happy."

Delgado's expression didn't change but his foot began to dance over his knee. "You get around."

"Enough. Scott was out with Katy on Saturday night."

By the look of surprise that crossed his face, I figured I had caught him off guard. Delgado's face registered another look of surprise. "How did you know that?"

"I'm a detective. I get paid to know things like that and I don't reveal secrets or sources. It isn't good for business."

Delgado smiled. It looked as if it was an effort; his face kind of divided into two planes with the lower half smiling while his eyes maintained their pained expression. The mark of a drinker was in Delgado's face, a lack of luster in his eyes and a slackness in the flesh around his mouth. He was young enough that it gave him a certain character now, but I knew what it would do to him in the coming years. I'd seen that in Matt Johnson's face earlier today, and there had been years of drinking when I had only to look in my own mirror to see the damage.

"Bren wants to hire you."

"What for?"

"To find out what happened to Katy."

"What's it to him? He was just a rich john she went out with occasionally. Why would he want to fork out more money now that she's dead?"

Delgado now looked completely grieved. "He liked her."

I shook my head. "A lot of people liked her. They're not barging in here at night hiring me to find out what happened to her."

"He wants to get it cleared up before it turns into a scandal."

"What scandal?"

Delgado shot a hand out, gripping his ankle until his knuckles turned white. "The police investigation."

"Who said there was going to be a scandal? And if there is, what's it got to do with Scott?"

Delgado put his foot on the floor and hissed, "Damn it, he's going to be questioned. The cops will be poking around in his business."

"So what? If he doesn't have anything to hide—"

"Bren doesn't need this kind of attention right now."

Raising my hands in a gesture of helplessness, I stared at him across the desk: Gideon Lowry, detective, trying to talk himself out of a job. "Hiring me isn't going to solve his problems. Maybe what he needs is a good lawyer."

Delgado shook his head. "You won't do it?"

"Why should I?" Letting an edge of anger creep into my voice. "There's a mystery surrounding Katy Morgan's death, a big mystery. But I don't know what it's got to do with Brendan Scott and you aren't telling me. You want to hire me to take the heat off someone I barely know. Why didn't Scott come in here himself?"

"He's out of town."

"See what I mean," I scoffed. "What are you, his slave?

You do his dirty work and then get fed the scraps off his plate."

Delgado stood up. His face was contorted with rage. "What the hell's that supposed to mean?"

"After he had dinner with Katy, Scott dropped her off at a hotel downtown where she met you."

Delgado glared at me as if I had bitten him.

"And don't ask me how I know that. Something happened between the two of you that night, an argument, a disagreement. Whatever you want to call it. But it changed her. She wasn't the same. And the next day she was dead. Now you want to hire me to find out what happened to her. You'd better come clean. Give me something I can work with. Otherwise, you know where the door is."

Delgado shifted on his feet for a moment, then sat back down.

"Katy had something that belonged to me. Well, to Bren and me really."

"What was that?"

"Some treasure we recovered."

"A wine chalice by any chance?"

Delgado straightened in his chair, leaning forward. His dead eyes suddenly came to life, damp and sparkling. "You know about it?"

I deliberately kept my own expression immobile, staring back into Delgado's excited eyes. "I've heard of it. How did Katy get possession of it if it was yours?"

"Do you know where it is?"

I shook my head. "I'm not playing this game with you. We'll be here all night. I asked you a question. Answer it and maybe we can get somewhere."

"She stole it."

"Like hell she did."

"She told you that, that it was hers? That tramp."

"Watch your mouth, Joe. There's an investigation under way. You don't want to be caught up in it."

Delgado pursed his lips together in a hurt pout. "You think I'd be in here hiring you if I was mixed up in her death in some way?"

"You haven't hired me, and you might do anything to get what you want if you're desperate enough."

Delgado shook his head, took a deep breath, and let a thin smile play over his lips as he eased back in the chair. "I see what you mean. You're no fool. I came to the right man."

"I've been a fool plenty of times and probably will be plenty more. But right now I'm smart enough to know when I'm being taken for a sucker." I got up and started to walk to the door.

Delgado didn't move. "No one's taking you for a sucker."

"Then give me some straight answers. *You* say Katy stole that wine chalice from you. *She* felt she had a claim to it since it was stolen when she got it. What's the truth?"

"Why did she hire you then?"

"There you go again answering a question with a question."

Delgado made a fist and, with his elbow on the chair arm, propped his chin on it. "Look, it was worth some money. Katy had it. I can't tell you any more because other people will be compromised, but she had it. It didn't belong to her. She was supposed to return it to me yesterday. I never heard from her. Now she's dead."

"How did Katy get it?"

Delgado looked dejected. "She took it from me, from my house."

"But you can't tell me why. Is that what you were arguing about Saturday night at the club?"

Delgado nodded. I sat back down behind the desk.

"And you want to hire me to do what? Find out why Katy's dead, find the missing chalice?"

"They're connected, aren't they?"

I shrugged. "Maybe. Maybe not."

Delgado hesitated. "Do you know where it is?"

"Maybe. Maybe not."

Delgado swept the air with his fist. "Damn it, we want it back."

"What's it worth to you?"

"You'll be taken care of."

"I mean what's the chalice worth?"

The corner of Delgado's mouth twitched. "A couple hundred grand. Maybe more."

I whistled. "A lot of dough."

"Some. Can we hire you?"

"Maybe. If you're willing to meet my conditions."

"What are they?"

"I'm looking to find out why Katy killed herself, if that's what happened. I want a hundred and fifty a day and expenses. And if I turn up the cup in the process, we'll negotiate a further settlement."

Delgado tried to smile. "I suppose that's reasonable."

I didn't care whether it was reasonable or not. I didn't like the smile or the way he spoke, but I took his money. I was working, being paid for something I had been doing for nothing. There was nothing wrong with that, but I had a queasy feeling in the pit of my stomach when he handed over five hundred dollars, and the feeling didn't go away with Joe Delgado.

13

◇

The drugstore hadn't yet opened when I got there the next morning a few minutes before seven-thirty. I purchased a newspaper from the vending machine outside and stood on the sidewalk reading it, waiting for the doors to be opened.

There was little traffic, the sun was bright, and with no sign of a breeze it carried the promise of a hot day. Across the street a kid stood in the shade beneath an awning, leaning against the outside wall of a convenience store, a cigarette in the corner of his mouth.

A few more people joined me on the sidewalk. A minute or so past the half hour a waitress unlocked the doors and we went in. A patron ribbed the waitress about the time. She swore in Spanish, but smiled. I sat at the counter, ordering a couple of scrambled with grits and sausage.

Five minutes before eight, I'd finished eating and had scanned the paper. Leaving a tip on the counter, I paid the cashier and went back out on the street. The kid was still hanging out across the way. I walked the few blocks up to the trailer park where Katy Morgan had lived. It was quiet, and for the moment at least it was cooler back here where the sun hadn't yet penetrated.

Around the narrow lane winding through the trailer park, a towheaded kid maybe seven or eight years old, his face smeared with freckles and dirt, careened astride a miniature bike that looked as if it had been cobbled together from various discarded parts cut down to peewee size.

I stood outside Katy's trailer. There was no yellow police tape, signaling, I assumed, that Bill Eberhardt had completed his investigation here.

"Don't nobody live there now, mister," the kid said, stopping his bike to watch me. He had on a grimy pair of shorts, no shoes or shirt. "Are you a cop?"

I shook my head as a woman's voice called in the distance. The kid inclined his head in that direction. "Gotta go," he said, leaning forward over the handlebars and pedaling fast while making a sirenlike sound.

Standing on the rickety steps, I knocked on the door and was surprised when it was opened. A woman in shorts and a T-shirt stood there, a rubber glove on one hand. She was probably in her midforties, her short dark hair flecked with gray. She had washed-out eyes and a birthmark staining the corner of one cheek.

"I was wondering about the status of the trailer."

"Can't help you. I was called in to clean it. I thought you was the manager. I got all this personal stuff boxed that I don't know what to do with."

On the floor behind her I could see the boxes containing Katy's belongings.

"Where's the manager?"

"The first trailer at the entrance."

I thanked her and walked back to the entrance to the park. The first trailer was somewhat larger than the others, but except for a waist-high picket fence that enclosed one side, it didn't appear to be in much better shape. Pushing open the gate, I walked up to a darkened screen door and called, "Hello."

"Yeah," a voice from inside said. "Who is it?"

"I was down at Katy Morgan's trailer and the cleaning woman said I could find the manager here."

"Got nothing available."

"I'm not looking to rent. I wanted to ask you a couple of questions about Katy Morgan."

"Jesus H. Christ. Ain't I done with answering questions about her?"

I didn't say anything. Finally, the voice's body materialized inside the unopened screen door: a big paunchy guy with little hair and suspenders holding up shiny slacks over a faded blue wash-and-wear shirt. "You a cop?"

"Private."

"Yeah, I recognize you now. I seen you here the day they found Katy."

"I was wondering if Katy had a lot of visitors."

"Not so many. She lived pretty quiet back there. She'd get herself all dolled up once in a while, and went out whorin' around, I reckon, but she never brought 'em back here."

"No boyfriends?"

"Not that I seen. She paid her rent on time. I didn't keep tabs on her, but I'm tellin' you I never saw men comin' in here to see her. Some women now and then, but no men."

"What about her neighbors?"

"The cops already talked to 'em. On one side of her is an old woman practically deaf and half-blind, got a TV and the air conditioner going all day, and on the other side a guy works nights."

"What about her stuff?"

"Far as I heard, they ain't found no kin. I'll turn it over to the police or the Salvation Army."

From the trailer park I decided to walk over to the courthouse. It was only a few blocks, giving me time, I reasoned, to figure out what I was going to say to my old friend Webb Conners, who was a bailiff with the sheriff's department.

Lurking across the street when I came out of the trailer park was the same lanky youth I'd seen earlier holding up the wall to the convenience store.

At the courthouse I walked up two flights of stairs and then stood on the front balcony looking down on the street and the courthouse lawn. The lanky youth was loitering in the shade of the huge ficus tree.

Inside the courthouse, the sweat I'd worked up dried quickly in the cold air-conditioning. I made my way to the clerk's office where a sloe-eyed secretary sized me up before returning her gaze to the computer screen. "Webb's in Courtroom A," she said.

Courtroom A was Just Watson's court. A half dozen prisoners in orange jumpsuits sat shackled together in the jury box awaiting arraignment. The judge glanced up when I came in, nodding in my direction.

Webb stood in one corner near the jury box, leaning against a doorjamb, one forearm resting atop the butt of his pistol encased in the stiff leather belt around his ample waist. He looked at me and, without expression, lifted his hand and laconically pointed a finger toward me.

I took a seat in the gallery behind the railing that separated the spectators from the court proceedings. Five minutes later when the judge summoned the lawyers for a conference at the bench, I stood up and approached the railing nearest to Webb.

Pushing himself away from the doorjamb, Webb slowly ambled over, lowering his head so that I could whisper to him. "I need to talk to you. When will you be free?"

Webb turned to look at the prisoners. "One more to go. Twenty minutes max."

"Meet you at the café?"

Webb nodded.

I went out and wandered down to Yesterday's, the café frequented by the courthouse crowd. I ordered coffee. I was halfway through a cup when the lanky youth came in and sat at the counter. I didn't pay him any attention. A few minutes later Webb sauntered in and spread his uniformed bulk in the seat opposite me in the booth I'd taken. "What say, Bud?"

"See the kid sitting at the counter?"

Webb turned and looked.

"Recognize him?"

"Nope. Why?"

"He's been tailing me all morning."

"I can take him in if you want and run a computer check on him."

I shook my head. "I'll handle it."

"You on a case, Bud?"

I nodded. "And your name came up."

Webb had put on weight since I had last seen him, and his hair was turning gray and thinning. His face was full and fat, but hidden in the folds of flesh I thought I could still detect the kid I had known in high school. "I win the lottery or something?" Webb grinned.

"Not quite. Your name was on a list of clients who frequented Valentine's Escorts."

Webb's grin faded. A waitress came over and Webb asked for a glass of milk and some Key lime pie. I could fairly hear the nerve endings sizzle in his stomach. He glanced around when the waitress left. "Bud, what is this?"

"One of Val's girls died."

"I know that. Where'd you see my name?"

"That's not important. What is important is that the police investigation may spread out."

A patina of sweat dimpled Webb's hairline. The waitress put a glass of milk in front of him. "Sweet Jesus! Judy finds out, she's going to kill me. And don't look at me like that."

I smiled. "I'm not your accuser. The fire goes out between you and Judy, you want to stoke it a little, that's your business. Did you know her?"

"Who?"

"Katy Morgan, the girl who died."

Webb looked despondent. "I don't think so. Bud, I swear to God it was a couple of times. That's all."

I shrugged.

"We've been together a long time." He was of course talking about his marriage to Judy.

"You two having problems?"

"Bud, look at me. I'm getting old, I'm overweight, I've got a ticker that could go at any time."

"Webb, nothing's happened yet."

"Judy finds out—"

"Relax. She's worried about you. She knows something's wrong."

"Who told you that?"

"Peggy. I saw her the other day and she asked me to talk to you. Judy had confided in her. Look, if she hasn't heard anything yet, chances are good she isn't going to."

Webb remained dismal.

"I'd like you to do something for me."

"Sure, Bud."

"See what you can dig up on a couple of guys by the name of Brendan Scott and Joe Delgado."

Webb nodded, writing the names down in a notepad he took from his pocket. "Who are they?"

"They're in the treasure-salvage business. And they both knew Katy. Dig around in the courthouse and see if there's any paper on them."

"I'll do that for you, Bud."

"Thanks." I finished my coffee and got up to leave.

"Sweet Jesus," Webb said, but he stayed where he was, staring into his empty milk glass.

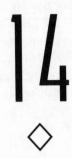

B ill Eberhardt dropped in shortly after the lunch hour. He was wearing the same striped tie with a wash-and-wear shirt similar to the one he'd been wearing when I had last seen him at Katy Morgan's trailer. He was alone.

"Hello, Bill." I grinned. "What brings you out in the midday heat?"

Sweat stains darkened the underarms of his shirt as he pulled a handkerchief from his back pocket and mopped his face with it. He stood in the center of the room directly beneath the overhead fan.

"I'm getting some pressure."

"Oh, what kind of pressure?" I leaned back in my swivel chair, lacing my fingers together. This was going to be interesting.

"From the department. They know you were out with the Morgan girl a couple of nights before she died."

"Well, that's true enough," I said pleasantly. "I never hid that fact."

"And then you happen to be the one to find her body."

"True, too."

Eberhardt mopped another round of sweat. His face was red and I didn't think all of it came from the heat. "Come on, Gideon, level with me. There are forces in the department that would like to bring you in for questioning."

I smiled. "Sure they would."

"I agreed to talk to you. Make life easy for me. For both of us."

"Sit down, Bill. You look uncomfortable standing there. What do you want to know?"

He pulled the wicker chair over so it was more directly under the fan and sat.

"What was your connection with her?"

Clasping my hands together, I pinched my upper lip between extended forefingers. "You know, Bill, between you and me, there were probably a few other names associated with Katy Morgan who would be less than happy to have their identities revealed. Am I right?"

He stared at me without expression. "You know you are."

I nodded. "So I guess it would make life easy, as you say, for me to tie this all up and hand it to you."

"Now, Gideon, you know better than that—"

"Do I? You just said you were feeling the pressure. Nobody in the department wants to get the town all lathered up over one dead hooker. Right?"

"I didn't say that."

"You'll concede my point though. A lot of people would be sleeping better if this just went away."

Eberhardt grimaced. "If it makes you happy, Gideon, I'll go along with you."

I gave him my friendliest smile and said, "Nothing

about this case makes me happy. I'm sorry to disappoint, but I can't tie it up for you."

"Just tell me what you had going with her."

"She had something, something that didn't belong to her, and she asked my advice on how to handle it. I think she was afraid she might be in some danger. I'm afraid I wasn't much help to her. I went over there on Sunday to talk to her about it."

Eberhardt seemed visibly relieved. "Care to give me the details?"

I shook my head. "Sorry, Bill, but it's an ongoing case."

"Your client is dead."

"I've got another client."

A hint of worry crept back into Eberhardt's eyes. "Are they connected?"

"My client and Katy?"

Bill nodded.

"They knew each other. Socially."

Bill took a deep breath, held it for a while before breathing again. "You're not on firm ground here, Gideon. You know that, don't you?"

"I'm doing my job. You're doing yours."

"Can we cooperate?"

"I'm cooperating."

"What was the piece of property?"

"A cup."

"A cup?"

"Yeah, something to drink out of."

"What was so special about it?"

"Part of the loot found on one of the treasure ships."

Bill puckered his lips thoughtfully. "Now we're getting somewhere."

"No, we're not, because that's as much as I'm going to say right now."

Eberhardt scratched his ear. "You don't see any connection between that cup and Katy's death?"

"I don't even know how Katy died."

"The coroner says it looks like suicide. There's no indication of murder."

Again, I saw her there on the kitchen floor, the skimpy robe barely covering her nude body; her skin had a bluish tint and the smell of the gas was nauseating. It wasn't a pretty picture and it didn't get any prettier with the realization that she'd died quickly. I shook my head, pinching the bridge of my nose as I tried to rid myself of the image of Katy in those last few minutes of her life.

When I raised my head, I could see moisture glistening on Eberhardt's upper lip. "Another thing you might be interested in. Katy had sex not long before she died."

Something turned over in my gut and a sour taste worked its way up the back of my throat. Val said that she didn't have Katy booked on Sunday, so whomever she was with was not linked to the escort service. I found an antacid tablet in the drawer of my desk and swallowed it.

"If it was suicide, why don't you just close the book on it? Why all the interest?"

Eberhardt shook his head. "No doubt we will. We'd like to tie up some loose ends. Like family. Who to notify. That sort of thing."

"She didn't have one."

"How do you know that?"

"She told me."

"She was kind of young, wasn't she? To not have a family."

I shrugged.

"Then there's your continued interest."

"My interest is personal at this point."

Eberhardt nodded. "I see. Except for that cup and your new client."

"Look, Bill, if it turns out that there is a link between Katy's death and the cup, I'll be the first to let you know."

"Where's the cup now?"

"No one seems to know."

"And you still won't say who your client is?"

I shook my head no. Bill sat immobile for a few minutes staring at me, then got up and ambled over to the front door, where he paused and looked back at me as if he had something important he wanted to say. But all he finally said was, "Ah, to hell with it," and walked out into the heat.

T he party at the judge's was small and informal and well under way by the time I got there shortly before eight. As it had been the other evening when I was there for dinner, the place was lit up, and Ardis, in a festive mood, greeted me when I walked up the flagstone path to the front porch. She wore a revealing white dress with wide shoulder straps and a lace front.

"Gideon, I was beginning to wonder if you were even coming. Just said you weren't much of a partygoer." She was all fluttery, kissing me on the cheek, but her eyes still didn't look directly at me. Maybe someone more interesting was just over my shoulder.

"Well, I wouldn't have missed this one. How's the judge?"

Ardis's laugh was throaty and happy. "Oh, somewhat uncomfortable, I think, but he'll survive."

I thought we were going inside and opened the screen

door to let her in, but Ardis motioned me away. "I want you to meet my son. He's over here. Patrick?"

I looked back along the porch and noticed a young man sitting alone in the shadows on a deck chair. He made no movement to come to us, so I followed Ardis over to where he sat.

"Patrick, this is Gideon Lowry. He's a relative of Just's. You'll like him. He's a private detective and he plays piano in a nightclub downtown."

I offered my hand and Patrick took it without getting up, barely glancing in my direction.

"He arrived late yesterday. He's still adjusting," Ardis said in a maternal tone. But her smile was stiff.

"I'm all right," Patrick said, but a hint of a whine was in his voice.

"Well, bored maybe, hanging out with the old fogies. You don't have to hang around here if you don't want. Why don't you go downtown? Take the car if you like." Ardis stood beside him, her hand caressing the hair that curled over his shoulders.

"I'm fine."

Ardis stared at him for a moment as he sat in the darkness, a drink in his hand. Perhaps he was drunk, I thought, which would explain, if not excuse, his rudeness.

She turned and we walked into the house together. Once inside the door, she put her hand on my arm, stopping me. "Don't mind Patrick. He's just going through an awkward phase right now."

Awkward phase struck me as odd for someone almost twenty. I wondered if it wasn't something else. "Have he and Just spent any time together?"

Ardis shook her head. "Very little. Just has tried, but he hasn't had a lot of experience with a kid that age."

It wasn't my place to say that Patrick wasn't a kid any longer, that it was time to deal with him as an adult, but it didn't stop me from thinking it.

Ardis smiled. "It'll work out, I'm sure."

We went into the living room where Just was tending bar. Ardis introduced me to a couple of older winter residents of Key West whom I didn't know. I bantered with them for a moment, then made my way to the bar. Everyone here was in expensive threads, looking as if they had all the comfort money could buy.

"Club soda with a twist?" Just asked.

I nodded, watching him pour the fizzy water, then pick up a knife to cut a lemon. "Damn!" Just said suddenly.

"What?"

"I nicked myself." He lifted his hand, wrapping a napkin, which was already turning red, around the cut on his finger.

He left the bar and I followed him outside to the back porch and into the kitchen where he ran cold tap water over the cut, trying to stem the bleeding. It seemed to bleed for a long time.

Just got a paper towel and wrapped his finger again. "I'm a little edgy. The business with Katy, getting married, Ardis's son . . . ."

"You having some doubts?"

"The heebie-jeebies. It'll pass."

We stood there a moment silently, Just staring out the window into the night. He seemed reluctant to rejoin the party. "Joe Delgado came to see me yesterday."

"Delgado." Just said the name as if trying to identify it. "Delgado. The name's familiar."

"He's a treasure salvor."

Just nodded. "Right. He's been in court a couple of times. A problem with drinking and driving. In fact I think he's on the calendar again soon, and this time I'll probably throw the book at him. What did he want with you?"

"To hire me to look into Katy Morgan's death."

Just turned away from the window. "What's his involvement with her?"

"He was out with her last Saturday night. I saw them together after I left here. They were arguing."

"What about?"

"I don't know. But I had the feeling that's what Katy wanted to talk about when she called me. There anything personal between you and Delgado? Or his backer, Brendan Scott?"

Just thought about it for a moment. "Scott? No, I don't think I know him. Is there any connection between them and that missing cup you told me about?"

"There might be, but if there is, I haven't made it yet. I'd like to know more about Delgado."

"I wish I could help you, Bud, but other than the times I've encountered him in court, I don't really know him."

"Know who?" Ardis had just come in.

"Some treasure hunter Bud was telling me about."

"Oh. Well, right now there are a bunch of people lined up at the bar wanting a drink. We wondered where the bartender had disappeared."

Just looked down at his finger.

"Justice, what happened?" Ardis came over and examined Just's finger.

"I cut it a minute ago. It's okay now. I can go back to work."

Ardis looked at me and shook her head. I followed them into the house. The crowd had grown. They appeared to be mostly winter residents, no one I knew well.

I wondered what the total net worth of this crowd was as I watched Ardis move among them, apparently at ease, something I had a feeling her husband-to-be wasn't. Ardis clearly liked this sort of life, and I couldn't help wondering how the judge was going to adapt after so many years of solitude.

I moved around, eavesdropping on conversations. "Do you know the Holloways?" I overheard Ardis ask a woman.

"Well, yes, I had lunch with Connie the other day. We're both on the Historic Preservation Board."

"I'd love to meet her."

"She's very busy but maybe the three of us could have lunch next week."

"That would be wonderful." Ardis turned and saw me. She looked embarrassed, as if I had caught her at something.

Moving on, I had a few abbreviated conversations, and after half an hour I had had enough. I started to go out on the porch, but stopped at the screen door when I heard voices. The judge's voice and Patrick's.

"You're not my father. You can't tell me what to do."

"I was making a request, not telling you." Just's voice was placating.

"Don't waste your breath."

After a moment's silence, footsteps descended the steps. A moment later a car door slammed. I went back inside and found Ardis. "I'm going to leave now."

"Oh, don't do that. It's still early and you're the only one I really know here." She guided me over to the bar. "We're running low on ice. Just was going to ask Patrick to go and get some."

I didn't say anything. Ardis fixed herself another drink. "I wonder where he is."

"I'll take a look for him."

I went on the porch. Just wasn't there and neither was Patrick.

Thinking I'd stay at least until the judge returned, I sat down in the deck chair in the shadows and waited.

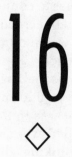

16

◇

T he muffled sounds and jumbled chatter of the party drifted to the porch where I sat staring up at the sky through the ragged edges of palm fronds towering over the front porch. I thought about the judge and Katy Morgan and Joe Delgado and Brendan Scott.

On the surface it all seemed so simple. Katy had a chalice recovered from a treasure ship that was worth some money. Apparently, she had taken or stolen it from Joe Delgado—why remained a mystery. Because it didn't belong to her, she was worried enough to hire me to protect her, but before I could do anything, she was dead. What complicated matters was that I didn't know if her death was connected to that wine chalice. She was depressed. Was that because of her life, her father, the chalice—or all three?

Then there was Katy's connection to the judge, his relationship with her mother, and his reluctance to tell Ardis. I couldn't figure that, even as private as he was; it would have seemed easier to confess and get it over with, especially if he was so concerned that Ardis might find out on her own. Patrick was another wrinkle. He bothered me. He bothered me a lot. Clearly he didn't want his mother to marry. That was making it tough on Just—even tougher if Patrick were to find out about the judge and Katy's mother. Even if it was in the past. I thought about it some more and decided we needed to talk, the judge and I. Then I stopped thinking and just let my mind drift up there in the vast darkness. Which was where I was when a car pulled up out front; the sound of a car door slamming was followed by footsteps on the flagstones leading up to the house. Thinking it was the judge, I stood up to greet him.

Instead, I encountered a uniformed cop, someone I didn't recognize.

"Is this Judge Watson's place?" he asked me.

"It is. What's the problem?"

"It's the judge. He's been in an accident."

I felt a tightening in my chest, a prelude to worse news. "What kind of an accident?"

"His car ran off the road and struck a telephone pole."

Jesus! "How is he?"

"He's alive. He's been taken to the hospital. That's about all I know. Any of his family here?"

"His fiancée. I'll tell her and bring her to the hospital. You don't know anything more about the accident?"

"We're investigating right now. I was dispatched over here to inform the family."

"Thanks."

The cop saluted and went back down to the street and got in his car. I took a deep breath and went to find Ardis.

She was at the bar chatting breezily with a couple in matching plaid shirts. "I don't know what's holding Just up," Ardis said, seeing me. Something in my face must have alerted her. "Gideon, what?"

I took her arm and guided her out of hearing of the others to tell her what had happened.

"Oh, my God!" A hand went to her mouth. "Is he . . ."

"He's at the hospital. I'll drive you there."

A shudder went through her body; she closed her eyes for a moment, her fist pressed to her mouth. Then she straightened up and seemed to regain her composure. "I'll have to get everyone out. Where's Patrick?"

"I don't know. He isn't outside. I haven't seen him."

Ardis stepped to the center of the room and asked for everyone's attention, saying simply that Just had been in an accident and she was going to have to ask people to leave because she had to go to the hospital. She said that she hoped that it was simply a minor accident but that she didn't have any details.

The party was over. Ten minutes later I helped her close up the house, turning off lights and shutting doors. We made a brief search for Patrick until, on the way to my car, she realized that her own car was gone.

"I should leave a note." She went back to the house and returned moments later.

"Is Patrick staying here?"

"No, he's staying with me, but he might come here. Actually, my place is on the way. Could we pass by there and see if he's gone home?"

"Of course." I followed her directions. Ardis's house was three blocks from the judge's. The porch light was on when we stopped in front.

"The car isn't here," Ardis said. "He must be downtown someplace."

"Do you want to leave a note here, too?"

"No. If he comes back to Just's, he'll get that note. Otherwise I'll call him from the hospital, or see him when I get home."

We rode the rest of the way to the hospital in tense silence. When I looked over at her once, she was gripping her hands tightly in her lap.

At the hospital I parked in the lot nearest the emergency entrance. An ambulance was pulled up in front, and as we walked to the entrance, paramedics were removing a man on a stretcher, an IV attached to his arm. Glancing at the face on the stretcher as we hurried past, Ardis grimaced and clutched my arm.

At the reception desk, I introduced us as relatives of Just Watson's. The clerk disappeared for a moment, then returned to say that Just was in intensive care and in stable condition, but beyond that she didn't have any information.

Ardis and I tried to make ourselves comfortable in the plastic seats in the waiting room. The distant hum from the relentless fluorescent light did nothing to make the wait more bearable. A janitor pushed an electric buffer across the floor. The medicinal smells, the hushed, hurried steps of soft-soled shoes across the polished linoleum, the other distraught faces in the waiting room, combined to form a dismal setting.

Half an hour passed before a doctor appeared. Ardis and I both stood up. The doctor was young, but he looked as grim as the surroundings.

"How is he?" Ardis asked. She seemed tightly controlled.

"Well, he's alive. We don't yet know the extent of his injuries."

"But he's going to recover?"

"I would say so. He's in good shape for a man his age." The doctor flicked the top of a ballpoint pen as he spoke. "He was thrown forward. Hit his head on the windshield.

We haven't been able to determine yet if there's any neurological damage, or if he just suffered a concussion."

"What's the worst case?"

The doctor looked down at his feet. "Well, if there's nerve damage, there could be some paralysis."

"Paralysis?"

"Possibly. I just don't know yet. We're getting a specialist in first thing in the morning to look at him."

"Will he recover?"

"I hesitate—"

"Doctor," Ardis insisted, "give me the worst of it."

The doctor stared into Ardis's gray eyes. "Worst case, he won't walk again. But you must understand we don't know that now. We can't diagnose until he's seen by a specialist."

Ardis took my arm again, gripping it tightly. "I'd like to see him. We were going to be married tomorrow."

◇

Lying under the harsh glare of lights, his body hooked up to the usual intensive-care contraptions, the judge seemed diminished. His hair was matted, his face gray and sunken, his eyes closed and his breathing irregular. Standing beside the bed, Ardis grasped Just's right hand. His eyes remained closed. A tear swelled and slowly leaked down Ardis's cheek. I stood beside her, waiting, seeking some sign that the judge was aware of our presence. None came.

"This is so terrible," Ardis said. "We had so much planned."

"I know. I'm sorry." There seemed to be nothing else to say.

Ardis stroked the judge's hand, repeating his name over and over again. "Justice . . . Justice." There was no response.

I offered to drive Ardis back to her place, but she said, no, she'd rather stay at the hospital, so I left her there, telling her I'd check with her first thing in the morning and asking her to call me if she had any news. Then I drove to the accident site on Flagler Avenue.

Just's car had been removed and nothing except a little shattered glass in the roadway indicated anything unusual had happened. I parked, got out of the car, and stepped over the curb to the concrete pylon that Just's car had struck.

Along here, Flagler was a four-lane street separated by a median, and traffic commonly sped along at thirty or forty miles an hour. A convenience store was fifty yards or so behind where the car had slammed into the pylon, so presumably Just would already have purchased the ice and been on his way home when the accident occurred.

I don't know what I'd expected to find here. Some isolated clue perhaps, too small for the police to have noticed, that would explain how this could have happened. To my knowledge the judge had not been a fast driver, or a reckless one. Somewhat preoccupied, yes. The memory of Willa's accident so many years ago must surely have been stamped on his subconscious. Of course, the irony of having history repeat itself now, of all times, did not escape me.

There were no clues. Nothing more than the late-night traffic passing, people staring out their windows at me as I knelt in the grass beside the pylon searching for something, anything. At the corner the traffic lights switched from red to green with monotonous regularity, and in the distance, towering over the baseball diamond, lights lit up the field where a game was in progress.

Just's car was a later-model Oldsmobile, nothing too sporty, a solid sedan, one that I knew the judge, with his meticulous habits, kept in good running order. His boat engine was checked and serviced a couple times a year, as was the car.

Just must not have been wearing his seat belt if, as the doctor said, he had struck his head on the windshield. I stared at the traffic, pondering how he could have gone up over the curb and hit this pylon unless the Oldsmobile had gone out of control due to a mechanical failure, or unless Just had had a heart attack, which the doctor hadn't indicated. Or unless he had been trying to avoid a potentially more serious accident. The latter had been at the back of my mind soon after the cop had shown up at the house with the news.

I got in the car and drove downtown to police headquarters where I asked the dispatcher if she could locate the officers who had investigated the accident involving Just Watson on Flagler earlier in the evening. She said, yes, that one of them was on his break at a café on Truman. I looked at my watch.

It was almost ten-thirty. I went out to the car and drove over to the café. The traffic cop sat alone at a corner table, eating a burger and reading a magazine. I introduced myself and asked if I could join him for a moment to talk about Judge Watson's accident.

"Sure, sit down."

It was too late for coffee, but I hadn't had any dinner and realized I was hungry. I ordered scrambled eggs with home fries and coffee.

"Too bad about that," the cop said. "I didn't know him all that well, but he seemed like a good guy. I hear he was supposed to be getting married tomorrow."

I nodded. "Any idea what happened?"

The cop shook his head. "Not a lot of traffic along there what with the ball game going on and a weeknight. But someone happened to look out the window of one of the twenty-four-hour joints and said it looked like another car was speeding and forced the judge off the road. I just don't know how reliable that information is, however."

"Why not?"

"The guy was nearly fifty yards away, looking out a window at an angle to the accident. And he'd been drinking."

"That was the only witness?"

"The only one we found so far."

"You get a description of the other car?"

The cop shook his head. "Something red and sporty. That's all."

"Any marks on the judge's car?"

"Didn't appear to be, but we're looking into that."

I ate my eggs when they came, chatted some more with the cop but without getting any further information before he finished and left. My own appetite had suddenly disappeared.

18

◇

The night was balmy. Away from the bump and grind of downtown I cruised the residential streets, where it was quiet as a church on Monday morning. There was a light flutter of air through the foliage along with the distant and muted murmur of insects. Even the Buick seemed to honor the silence, its motor purring without its usual knock and rattle. Rolling slowly past the judge's, I looked at his darkened house.

The homes along here combined prankishness and stateliness, the gingerbread trim like figments of some architect's wicked imagination. Prowling the streets, I was all too aware of my destination. At Ardis's place, I slowed to a crawl, creeping past on threadbare tires that whined faintly against the still-warm asphalt. The house was dark, no car out front. I crept on, went around the block, came back, and parked half a block away, under the spreading branches and feathery leaves of a tamarind tree.

The clock on the dash, still functioning after twenty

years, read fifteen minutes before midnight. I settled back to wait, wait and think about Just lying in a hospital bed, wondering what had happened to him.

I didn't wait long. A few minutes after midnight the quiet was broken by a car tearing down the street, fast, tires squealing as it braked sharply and pulled up in front of Ardis's. The car was new, something foreign, sporty, a hatchback, and from the spreading light of a streetlamp on the corner, I could see its mirrored finish and bright red paint job.

The interior light came on as the car door opened, and I caught a glimpse of Patrick's sullen face just before he got out, slamming the door and marching somewhat unsteadily into the house. Lights came on. I waited another fifteen minutes, then left the Buick and walked to Ardis's car and examined the exterior side panels, feeling the smooth metal against my hand. There were no dents or damage to the paint.

The lights were still on in the house, and as I started to walk up the sidewalk, a blast of music came from the open windows, something raucous, calculated to destroy the serenity of the night.

The front door was open. I didn't bother knocking, just walked into the front room, pausing to note the comfortable but modest furnishings, a clear reflection of Ardis's style. The music coming from the back of the house grew louder as I made my way through the dining room and into the kitchen, where Patrick stood at the counter, his back to me, his scrawny body pulsing to the beat while he fixed himself a sandwich.

The tape player was on top of the refrigerator just to my left, and I reached up and pushed the off button, hearing the jagged whine of the tape as the noise faded.

Patrick jumped as if he had been jolted by an electric

shock. He turned, saw me, and said, "What are you doing, man? Who let you in here?"

"I let myself in, Patrick, just walked in the door."

Something in my voice must have sent a warning through him. He seemed to retreat somewhere inside himself. "What do you want?" He sounded like a little boy.

"I want to know where you were tonight, Patrick, when you left the party at the judge's house. I want to know what time you left and every place you've been tonight and everyone you've talked to. In short, buddy, I want the details of your life for the past three or four hours."

"Something wrong?" He stared at the floor. He was tall and skinny with thick, dark hair that curled over his ears and onto his shoulders. He wore a couple of thin gold hoops in one ear. He had on thick-soled shoes and baggy pants and a shirt that had a couple of tears in it. Maybe he was a hipster or a rocker or a grunge kid or whatever they called themselves these days. And maybe he was a punk; punks had always been the same.

"Yeah," I growled, "something's wrong all right. Where were you?"

"I hit a couple of the clubs downtown, I don't even remember their names, had some drinks, and moved on."

"All by your lonesome, too, I suppose."

"I don't know anybody here."

"And you didn't meet anyone?"

"I danced in one place."

"With anyone in particular?"

Patrick shook his head, refusing to look at me. "Just a lot of people out on the floor."

"You don't talk much, do you, Patrick?"

He shrugged.

"Would you say that you're antisocial?

"No. Why?"

"Because that's how you act. Like you've got a chip on

your shoulder. You barely spoke to me when your mother introduced us this evening, and you were offhand with her. What's the problem?"

Another shrug.

"You pissed because she's getting married to the judge?"

Patrick looked up. "You've got no right coming in here. I don't have to answer your questions."

"You a mama's boy, Patrick? Is that what it is? You think you're going to lose her?"

He charged across the room flailing his gangly arms. I grabbed one of them. "Take it easy." He struggled a little more, then went limp. "Let's sit down and have a chat." I led him over to the table and pulled out a chair. He didn't want to sit. I pulled out another chair and straddled it. "Did you see the judge leave the house during the party?"

No answer. I let the silence hang.

Patrick finally said, "I'm going to bed."

I didn't say anything. Patrick didn't move.

"What do you want, man?"

"You to answer a couple of questions. If you don't, I'm going to call the cops and your mother." That got his attention.

"What for?"

"Because you saw the judge leave the house this evening, didn't you, Patrick?"

"So what?"

"And you left right after that, following him, didn't you?"

Patrick stared at the floor.

"They identified your car. It's just a question of time before you're answering these questions down at the police station. You're better off talking to me."

He sniffled.

"Why'd you follow him?"

"I don't know."

"You don't know? You just follow people without a reason?"

Patrick stared at the floor. "I saw the accident, man."

"What accident?"

"The judge. I saw the whole thing. He ran off the road."

"And you ran him off, didn't you, Patrick?"

"No. I swear it."

"Patrick, there was a witness. Someone identified your car."

His shoulders heaved involuntarily. "I didn't," he sobbed. "I really didn't."

"Take it easy, then, and tell me what happened."

He sat down at the table, burying his head in his arms, and cried. I waited. When he was finished, Patrick got up and washed his face at the sink, drying it on a tea towel. He wouldn't look at me. "What's going to happen to me?"

"I don't know, Patrick. That depends. Why don't you tell me what happened."

He wasn't a talker, Patrick. Words just seemed to stick in his throat somewhere as if it were a struggle for him to articulate the simplest feeling or relate the details from an incident as recent as this evening's. Whether it was embarrassment and humiliation or his natural reluctance to express himself, I couldn't tell. But what emerged was a hesitant, confused jumble filled with long pauses and false starts. I tried to prod him with questions, but that didn't seem to help either.

He admitted to following the judge. Even, as much as I could coax out of him, to having some kind of fantasy in which the judge would have an accident, nothing fatal, just a metal cruncher, a fender bender that would lay him up for a while, delaying the wedding.

But there wasn't much traffic, and all it was, was a

fantasy. Patrick had had a few drinks, but he wasn't drunk. At some point he decided to forget it and made a move to pass the judge; maybe he'd gunned the engine a little, but nothing reckless. Then he didn't know what happened. He downshifted, looked in his rearview mirror, and saw the judge up on the curb, the nose of the Oldsmobile buried in a concrete pylon. Patrick burned some rubber getting out of there. That's all there was to it. He'd done nothing to cause the judge to go off the road like that. It really wasn't his fault, Patrick said.

When it happened, he had gotten scared because he'd been thinking about something like that and then it had just happened. It scared him because he'd been drinking and somehow, with his twisted logic, he believed it was his fault even though he knew he hadn't done anything except think about it. He didn't want to hang around, so he had peeled out, gone downtown, and gotten drunker. And felt guiltier. So by the time I showed up and began questioning him, he had pretty much convinced himself that he was guilty.

At least that was what I pieced together. He sat down again at the kitchen table, his head lowered, never looking at me, occasionally glancing around the kitchen, startled by the least noise.

"Is he dead?"

"No, he isn't dead. But he's in bad shape, maybe even paralyzed."

"Shit. It wasn't my fault." Patrick turned away, his expression morose.

"Maybe not. But what do you have against him?"

Patrick shook his head. "I don't know. He's too old," he mumbled.

I felt like reaching out and grabbing a handful of his hair and lifting his head from the table, but instead I stared at him. Patrick looked back at me blankly.

"You probably don't deserve him. Come on. Let's take a ride."

"What for?"

"We're going someplace."

"I don't want to go anywhere."

"You don't have any choice."

"Where? You're not going to turn me in, are you?"

"No. I'm not. I'm going to give you a history lesson."

Patrick seemed visibly relieved and stood up.

We walked out and I closed the door behind us. "It won't be as much fun, but we'll go in my car."

I hustled him over to the Buick and got him into the passenger side, then walked around the front of the car and got behind the wheel. The Buick gave out a high-pitched whinny of protest when I started it.

"Where we going?"

"You'll know when we get there."

Patrick hunkered down in the seat, folding his arms across his chest in a gesture of defiance. I turned onto the boulevard, following it along the water until it intersected US 1, taking that route out of town and heading up the Keys. It was one o'clock in the morning, a weeknight, with hardly any traffic. Once we were beyond the lights of the convenience stores and the all-night gas stations, the road turned into a dark ribbon bisecting two bodies of water, and soon there was just the road and the sky and the stars and the water, and with the fresh smell of the sea on the rush of air coming in the open windows, I could almost forget the scared kid sitting beside me.

We drove in silence for twenty-five miles before I slowed down and took a right along a fill road bordered for a couple of miles by mangroves, then took a left onto another asphalt road, the original US 1, now used as an access to the homes that had been built along it after it ceased to be the main drag. I crept along, the lights on high beam, searching the roadside until I came to an old, thick-trunked seagrape tree. I pulled over and stopped the car, leaving the motor running and the lights on.

"Get out."

Patrick looked startled. He rubbed his eyes, staring out into the darkness at the tree illuminated in the glare of the headlights.

"What for? Where are we?"

"We're where I want to be." I got out, walked around to Patrick's side, and opened the door.

He stared up at me; his face, backlit by the reflection of lights, looked terrified. There was nothing here, just the car and the tree and the darkness and the smell of the distant sea. He got out.

"Go stand over there by that tree."

"What are you going to do?"

He was trembling. I pushed him forward until he was backed up against the tree. "Now, I'm going to tell you a story. A long time ago a woman died in a car wreck after hitting this tree. She was pregnant. She was driving from Key West just like we did except she was on this road, which was the only road along here at the time. She was on her way to visit friends who lived farther up the Keys, and she and her baby were killed when she drove her car into that tree to avoid an accident with another car that was driven by a drunk."

Patrick didn't say anything, just kept his head down and his back pressed against the tree.

"You want to know what that's got to do with you, I'll tell you. The woman who was killed was Just Watson's wife, and they'd only been married a couple of years."

I let him take that in for a moment. Then I told him something about Just's life since the accident, filling in the intervening years with a portrait of a man whose life would never be the same, a man who was changed in the instant it took for a car to plow into a tree.

"Two people were killed in that accident, but something in the judge died, too, and stayed dead for all these years. In fact, until he met your mother."

Patrick looked up, staring into the headlights like a trapped animal.

"Don't tell me about the judge being too old for your mother. You're just damned lucky to be getting him for a father, if you do get him. Now I'm going back into town. You want a ride, you can come along, or you can spend the night out here. Frankly, I don't give a damn one way or the other."

Patrick got in the car. I backed around and drove back over to the main highway, turning on the radio and finding some late-night jazz. Patrick didn't say anything on the ride into Key West, just sat bolt upright, staring straight ahead.

19

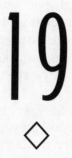

It was close to three o'clock by the time I got home. Patrick had said nothing when I dropped him off at his mother's. I wondered what he would tell Ardis, if he would say anything about the night's events. I really didn't care one way or the other. It had been a long day, and I was dog tired. I let myself in the back, avoiding the office and any more surprises that might have been on the answering machine.

Exhausted, I fell into bed, but sleep wouldn't come. I lay there in the dark thinking about the judge. How many times had I been in his car over the years? Too many to count, but none of those trips was particularly memorable except for the realization that Just Watson wasn't a particularly good driver. It wasn't that he drove fast, or recklessly, more that he was simply careless, talking or thinking about something that would often divert his mind from the routine attention it takes to drive a car.

It was odd, I thought, given the tragedy in his past, that

he should be a sloppy driver, but to my knowledge the judge had never had an accident until now. And I was convinced that it had been an accident, precipitated perhaps by Patrick's sudden, kidlike maneuver, leaving a distracted judge sufficiently startled that he drove into the pylon.

Was it Patrick's fault? Maybe, but it seemed like a pointless question now. It didn't stop me from thinking about it, though, until I finally drifted into a dreamless sleep only to be roused by the phone's ringing what seemed like a few moments later.

But it was seven o'clock by my watch as I stumbled into the front office.

"Sorry about the hour, Bud, but I tried you a few times last night and I wanted to get you before you went out."

"No problem, Webb."

"I heard about the judge. Is he going to make it?"

"We should know something this morning."

"It's awful what happened." Webb hesitated. "Bud, I thought you ought to know. The Katy Morgan thing. Bill Eberhardt's the lead investigator. You know him, don't you?"

"I've talked to him a few times already."

"That's what I wanted to tell you. They don't have any major leads. Katy Morgan's death was a suicide, but they seem to think there was something behind it and you're the key. They think you know more than you're letting on."

I didn't say anything.

"I'm just passing along what I've heard, Bud."

"And no doubt everyone's relieved. Including you."

"Bud, I—"

"It's all right, Webb. It isn't your problem." Webb topped out close to 250 pounds. I had a hard time picturing him in an intimate clutch with one of Val's girls. It was easier, and safer, to remember him across a pinochle table in the days when he and his wife, Judy, and Peggy and I were constant companions.

"Bud, if you think there's more to this, you know I'll do the right thing."

"You know damned well there's more to it, Webb. As far as this town's concerned, Katy was just another hooker who could embarrass the city fathers. It's a goddamned cover-up, the kind we're famous for, and it stinks."

"What about the judge?"

"What about him?"

There was a silence. "Forget it."

"Like hell I will. What are you trying to say?"

Another silence. Finally, Webb said, "There's a rumor the judge knew Katy Morgan, that he had some involvement with her."

I cut him off. "Well, you can scotch that one, Webb." There. Now I was even covering up for Just.

"I'm sorry." Webb's voice sounded distant. "If there's anything I can do, you know all you have to do is pick up the phone."

"Sure, Webb." There was a long pause before either of us hung up.

I punched on the answering machine and listened to the two messages from Webb the previous evening, and one from Val. It was too early to call Val so I got dressed and went out for breakfast. The newspaper had the story of Just's accident with some of the same history, minus the emotional drama, I had supplied Patrick with last night.

And of course there was no mention of Katy Morgan. She'd made the papers for a couple of days. Everyone involved with her had closed ranks to protect themselves, their reputations. It was despicable, and yet, in a way, by protecting the judge, I was part of the cover-up. It made me sick.

In the drugstore people stopped by my table and asked if I had more information. Everyone was genuinely concerned. The judge was a good guy with a solid reputation. No one asked about Katy Morgan.

I went home at nine o'clock and called Val, but got only her answering machine. I didn't leave a message.

Then I called the hospital and learned that Ardis had gone home earlier. I phoned her there. She said she had rested some, gotten cleaned up, and was getting ready to go back to the hospital. I told her I'd come over and take her there. Patrick wasn't mentioned.

When I got to her house fifteen minutes later, she was at the front door. I watched her walk down the sidewalk to the car. She had on a sundress and had done her best to make herself up, but she was looking her age.

"Did you talk to Patrick?" I asked when she got in the car.

"I tried to call him this morning from the hospital, but there was no answer. He was probably out late and is still asleep."

"I ran into him last night."

"Oh?" She looked across the seat at me.

"I think he had some misconceptions about Just. I tried to correct them."

"I was sure he would get over that once he'd spent some time here and gotten to know Justice. Now, I don't know what to think, or what to do."

"What about Just? Is there any change?"

"He's conscious. The doctor is supposed to be there later this morning."

Ardis had lost some of her spunk; her bounce was gone and she seemed confused and uncertain. I pulled into the unshaded hospital parking lot and left the car windows

open. We walked across the lot, the heat already beginning to build, and into the coolness of the air-conditioned
hospital.

Just was in a room on the third floor. We rode the
elevator up along with a nurse's aide who was attending
a wheelchair occupant.

Would Just be reduced to this? Ardis gazed down, and
I wondered if she was thinking about her honeymoon and
the plans she and Just had made for the rest of their lives.

He was in a private room, awake, his hair brushed back;
apart from the bandage on his forehead he looked to be in
better shape than I'd expected. Ardis bent to kiss him on
the cheek. When she straightened up, he said, "Sorry to
break up the party. You go out for a bag of ice and wind
up in here." He smiled. "Bud, come over here."

I walked around to the other side of his bed. "How are
you feeling?"

The judge took Ardis's hand. "The doctors aren't telling me anything. I feel like I have a bad hangover."

"They're going to run some tests this morning," Ardis
said.

"What kind of tests?"

"To make sure there isn't any permanent damage."

Just looked at me. There was nothing I could say.

"Ardis, I'd like to speak to Bud alone. Just for a
minute."

She forced a smile, withdrew her hand from Just's, and
went out of the room.

"Bud, this is a bitch. Do you know anything?"

"Not about your condition. Ardis was expecting to talk
to the doctor this morning."

"What about the accident? I don't have much of a memory of anything."

I had decided not to say anything about Patrick. We

123

could deal with him later. "You were probably forced off the road. It looks like it was an accident."

Just stared at me.

"I've looked into it and talked to the police. There isn't much to go on."

Just lifted his finger and motioned me closer. "Bud, I don't want Ardis to feel any obligation. She didn't buy into this. I want her to get on with her life. Talk to her for me."

I told him not to worry about Ardis and was about to tell him that she would stand by him when a nurse came in pushing a gurney, followed by Ardis. "Time for your tests, Judge Watson." The nurse smiled and I helped her lift him.

20

◇

I suppose he told you he didn't want me to go through this," Ardis said. "To feel that I had any responsibility to him."

We sat on a plastic-covered sofa in an alcove near the nurses' station. There was a table with some magazines, and opposite us a thin, vertical window that looked out over the city dump. A billowing plume of white smoke rose from one of the incinerator stacks there into the blue sky.

"Something like that," I replied.

"Does he think I don't know that? Listen, I'm not going to run out on him simply because he's had an accident and is temporarily disabled. If he's going to be in a wheelchair for a while, I'll be right behind him, pushing it."

"Why don't you tell him that?"

"Of course I'll tell him, but I'm not going to assume he won't walk again. And I don't want him to assume it either. No matter what the doctors say."

I smiled. Some of her spunk had returned, but she still had that nervous habit of constantly looking over my shoulder when she talked to me. A stray thought crossed my mind, and before I could wipe it away, I found myself wondering if she was speaking from a sense of duty or from conviction.

"I'm sure you'll have him on his feet in no time."

Ardis nodded. "Now, tell me, what else is going on?"

"What do you mean?"

"Gideon, do you think I haven't noticed? Every time I come into a room with the two of you, you stop talking or change the subject. Just has been behaving peculiarly. I know part of it was adjusting to the idea of marriage, but there's something more to it than that. Don't you think I should know what's going on?"

I stared at the smoke rising from the stack at the dump. "He had a personal problem he asked me to look into. It's been resolved."

"Did it involve another woman?"

"Just is the one you should ask."

"He's so reticent about his past."

I didn't say anything.

Ardis stared out the window for a moment, waiting, but I wasn't going to talk to her about Just's past. "I suppose I should call my son." She stood up, searching for a quarter in her handbag. I fished one from my pocket and handed it to her. "I'm going to go," I said. "I'll call this afternoon to get the results."

Ardis smiled and left in search of a phone.

On the drive back to town I wondered what Patrick would say to her, if he would tell his mother what had happened last night. Ardis seemed to be well-grounded, but she had a weak spot where Patrick was concerned; she was too ready to make excuses for him, I thought.

Family stuff that had been none of my business until last night.

At noon I stopped in the *grocería* next door and ordered a Cuban Mix sandwich. Looking out the screen door onto the street while I waited, I saw across the way the punk who had been dogging my movements.

The sandwich came hot and wrapped in wax paper, and I carried it home in a paper bag and ate it while standing in front of the kitchen sink. When I finished, I went into the office and raised one of the closed slats of the venetian blinds on the window overlooking Duval Street. Peering out, I could see the punk idly sauntering back and forth along the sidewalk across the street. I let the slat drop and went out the back door.

Winding my way through a couple of alleys, I worked back over to Duval Street, two blocks up from where I lived. Crossing, I went over another block, then came back via more lanes and alleys until I was standing beneath a shade tree between two buildings on the same side of the street where the punk was still loitering. When he passed by the tree, I stepped out and clapped a hand on his shoulder, putting just enough pressure on his tendon to let him know I meant business.

"What the hell!" the punk said.

"Let's take a walk."

"What for? I'm not doing anything."

"You're loitering. I can take you down to the police station and they'll turn your pockets inside out, run your name through a computer, and generally make life miserable for you for a few hours. You got anything you want to hide, you don't want to go through that. Or you can quietly walk across the street with me and sit down in my office, answer a few questions, and then be on your way. Suit yourself."

After a moment's hesitation, I felt the tension go out of

his body. We headed over to my place. I held the door open for him. He went in, glanced at the surroundings, then stood in the middle of the floor staring at me. "What do you want?" His eyes were focused on my chest. He was still trying to sound tough.

"I want to know why you're following me."

"Who said I was following you?"

"In the last twenty-four hours you've dogged me like wet on rain. And you've made no secret about it. So talk or I'll get the cops in to sweat it out of you."

"I got hired by somebody to watch you."

"Does somebody have a name?"

The punk shook his head. He couldn't have been more than twenty, twenty-one, wearing a dirty pair of jeans, run-down sneakers, and a T-shirt.

"Maybe a face," I suggested. "What did somebody look like?"

"I only talked to him on the phone. I never seen him."

"Yeah, and I suppose you get paid with a postal order."

The punk stared at me blankly.

"All right," I growled. "What are you supposed to do?"

"Keep track of who comes and goes."

I laughed. "You're a regular gumshoe, you are."

The punk just stood there without speaking.

"Get the hell out of here!" I barked. "And I don't want to see your face every time I look up, so make yourself scarce."

He ambled over to the door, opened it, then shot me the finger before he went out.

I leaned back in the chair and propped my feet on the desk. I was troubled, troubled by some nameless sense of urgency, a hollow core in the pit of the stomach combined with gastric pains I couldn't entirely attribute to the Cuban Mix sandwich.

The phone rang. "Bud?"

"Hello, Peggy."

"I just heard about the judge. It's terrible. What do you know about his condition?"

"Not a lot. They're running some tests. I should hear later this afternoon."

"It really is a tragedy, happening at this time in his life. Didn't it make you think of that other accident, Bud, when Willa was killed?"

"Yes, it did."

"It makes you wonder, doesn't it? I mean, it's almost like it was fate, or something. Don't you think, Bud?"

"I suppose that's one way of looking at it, Peggy."

"Well, what other way is there?"

"I don't know. Maybe I'm not as fatalistic as you."

Peggy was silent for a moment. When she finally spoke, her voice seemed filled with grief. "Oh, Bud, you're not suggesting someone could have done that deliberately, are you?"

"It was an accident, Peggy," I said curtly. "Nothing more." Then more gently: "I'll tell Just you asked after him."

"Is he going to retire?"

"I don't know. He was talking about it before this."

"I hope he does. If not, it will just make things worse."

"What do you mean?"

"You know the reputation he has for sentencing drunk drivers, Bud."

Probably over the years I'd heard rumors without thinking about them one way or the other. "Tell me."

"Always the max. No leniency. No excuses, and he's particularly hard on young people."

"No harm in that."

"No, but I wouldn't want to go before him now."

"I don't think you have to worry."

"No, but I think about my kids. They come home and

129

go out one night, get into a minor accident, and wind up spending a month, or whatever, in jail.''

"Tell them to take a cab.''

"That's exactly what I tell them. It doesn't do any good. They're kids.''

As if to say I didn't have kids, so what did I know? I thought about Patrick. Peggy talked for a moment more and then we hung up. I went back into the kitchen and stared down at Tom, who was contentedly washing himself in front of his empty food dish. What did I know? I didn't even like cats, and I was sharing my life with one.

I went out, got on my bicycle, and rode down to the docks.

21

◇

Joe Delgado was in the engine room of the old trawler with its twin elbow-shaped metal funnels attached to the stern—devices designed by the salvage industry to use the boat's prop wash to shift the sand along the ocean bottom and uncover whatever might have been buried there hundreds of years ago.

Delgado was changing fuel filters on the twin diesels. Standing on the deck, I stared down through the open hatch, breathing air thick with the smell of diesel fuel. Delgado had on a grimy T-shirt, his hands greasy as he tightened a nut on one of the fuel-filter cylinders. "Be right with you," he called up to me.

I walked over to the side, leaning against the gunwale. Garbage and debris had collected around the hull of the boat along the waterline. Moments later Delgado was on the deck beside me, the reek of diesel fuel still on his soiled clothes. He raised his arm and wiped sweat from his forehead on the sleeve of his T-shirt.

"One of these days I'll be able to hire someone to do this donkey work. What's up?"

"You've got a punk kid tailing me. I want him called off."

Delgado looked at me blankly. "Where'd you hear that?"

"He hasn't exactly been discreet about it. I surprised him and he told me he'd been hired to keep an eye on me. Who came and went from my office."

"And he says I hired him?"

"He didn't have to. I played Sherlock Holmes and deduced it was you. You're the only person who could care about who might be coming and going around me."

Delgado examined the grime beneath his fingernails.

"Look, Joe. I'm working for you. We've got to establish a certain amount of trust."

Delgado surprised me by looking up and grinning. "In my business that's a commodity in short supply."

"I told the punk and I'll tell you: I don't want to see his face anymore. The next time I look out the window and he's playing peekaboo with me, he's in for a rough time. And I'll hold you responsible."

"I don't know anything about it. If he's working for us, then it must have been Bren's idea. Bren's like that. He doesn't always let me in on his procedures. A matter of precaution and protection, I guess. You know, that chalice is worth a lot to him. To both of us."

"I know that punk couldn't protect a pea in a pod. And in case you've forgotten, I was hired to find out what happened to Katy, not that chalice."

"I thought we'd agreed they might be connected."

"Might."

Delgado didn't say anything.

"Judge Watson was in a car accident last night."

I tried to read something in Delgado's expression, but

nothing in his face or manner indicated that this information had any impact on him.

"He's going to be okay?"

"I'm waiting to hear."

"Why do I get the feeling that you're not just making conversation." Delgado's dark eyes narrowed. "Is that news supposed to mean something to me?"

"I said it was an accident."

"That's what you said. What I'm wondering is why you're telling me; what's it got to do with me?"

"Don't get excited. Maybe nothing. I just thought you ought to know."

"I don't like it." Delgado looked around irritably. "You make it sound like I'm under suspicion."

"Not at all."

"What happened to that business of trust you were talking about a minute ago?"

I shrugged. "It's just a commodity."

"If Bren was here, he'd tell you where you could put your commodities."

I smiled. "Bren's a tough guy, isn't he? But he isn't here though. It's just you and me."

"What do you want, Lowry?"

"I want to know about Katy Morgan. I think you know more about her than you're telling me. You're hoping I'm going to get my hands on that wine chalice and then your problems will be over, but I think your problems run deeper than that. It's time you leveled with me."

"We hired you to find out what happened to her. Why don't you do that?"

"I'm working on it. It would help if I had some idea why she was so despondent."

"Maybe because she had something that didn't belong to her."

"I've only got your opinion on that. You say she took it

133

from you. How many people knew she had that chalice? And who was she afraid of? You? Scott?"

Delgado's face turned red, his voice trembled. "Look, Katy had problems. A lot of problems. She was trying to sell it."

"The chalice? How do you know?"

"Because she tried to sell it back to us."

"Why didn't you just report it to the police then? She had stolen property and she was trying to fence it back to you."

"There were other claims on it, some dispute about it," Delgado said softly.

I nodded. "That's what Katy told me. Who else had a claim on it?"

"Look, we recovered it. We dug it out of the sand in twenty feet of water. It happened to be close to another salvage operation's dig where stuff was scattered for several miles. We found it. It's ours."

"Not now it isn't. Who else was Katy trying to sell it to?"

"I don't know. She never said. That's what we were arguing about Saturday night."

"So she was trying to get you to up the ante before she took it to another buyer? This puts you in a precarious position, Joe. The police are questioning me about that chalice, and about my client. So far I've been able to avoid them, but I don't know how much longer I can do that. I'm not in a good position here and I'll be damned if I'm going to let myself be hung out to dry just to keep your name out of it."

Delgado stared down at the garbage floating around the boat. He looked ashen. "What do you want me to do?"

"Give me some names."

"What names?"

"When you came to my office, you told me there were

people who would be affected if they knew that wine chalice was missing. Who are they?"

Delgado studied the ground. "Backers," he finally said.

"Financial backers?"

"Yeah. They've put up a lot of money. The chalice was collateral for some of it, but more importantly, if they know it's missing, we're going to have a hard time getting anything more. We need a bundle to operate this tub. We've got enough problems without that."

I nodded. "I'll say you do. So who are they?"

Delgado squirmed as if he were being tortured.

"Look," I said, "I don't need to reveal anything to anyone about the chalice, but I do need to know who's involved here, who the players are, if I'm going to do my job."

Delgado lifted his finger and pointed it at me. "I'm taking a hell of a risk. If this comes back to me, I'll deny everything."

"In your business that's what you do. You take risks and you don't trust anybody."

Delgado tried to smile. "Fred Pacey. And Tim Kelly."

I thanked him without expression, without acknowledging that the names meant anything to me. The beeper Delgado was wearing clipped to the waistband of his shorts sounded. He unclipped it, looked at it, and said, "I've got to make a call."

Delgado turned and I followed him over to a couple of pay phones. "Take it easy," I said. Delgado lifted the receiver on one of the phones, looking at me woodenly.

I got on my bike and rode off. Fred Pacey and Tim Kelly. I knew them casually, but more importantly I'd seen their names recently. Part of Val's clientele. Her secret clientele.

22

◇

Tourists were shuffling through the Treasure Museum, oohing and aahing over the gold, the Old World coins, the vast treasury of cargo that had been exhumed after several centuries from its underwater gravesite, cleaned up, and put on display—locked behind glass and Plexiglas. In one room a narrated video documenting a portion of the recovery played several times a day. Along the narrow corridor, winding like a maze through the windowless rooms, the air was thick with the smell of people, their sweat and cologne mingling with the musty metallic odors that had somehow permeated the barriers to the treasure. A gold bar reposed behind Plexiglas through which a circular hole had been cut wide enough to permit someone to reach in, heft the bar, and get an idea of its weight. The bar had been worn smooth where it had been grasped countless times, its touched surface glistening.

Uniformed guards looked on blankly while security cameras kept vigil over the people who studied the ancient contents within the locked cases. I wandered through the exhibit, saw some wine chalices, but nothing that matched the description Katy had given me of the stolen one.

In the gift shop near the exit I recognized Marjorie Blankenship, who was ringing up sales on the cash register. Marjorie had worked in the gift shop at the Hemingway House during a murder investigation I'd been involved in last summer at that tourist establishment. I waited while someone in front of me purchased a souvenir.

"Marjorie, I didn't know you were working here."

She looked up when I spoke, a smile spreading across her dimpled face. "Bud Lowry. What a pleasant surprise." Then, as suddenly as it appeared, the smile disappeared and Marjorie got a defensive look in her eyes. "There ain't going to be no trouble here now, is there? Like the last time I seen you at the Heme'nway House?"

I smiled. "I don't think you have to worry, Marjorie. I just need some information."

Although she didn't appear entirely convinced, Marjorie seemed to relax somewhat. The smile reappeared. She was a large woman with a round brown face and a neatly trimmed Afro flecked with gray. I had known her since I was a kid. "What sort of information you lookin' for, Bud?"

Without describing the wine chalice in any detail I gave Marjorie an idea of what I was looking for. When I finished, she picked up a couple of books on the counter that were for sale. "You might find something like that in one of these."

I took them and looked at the publication dates. "The thing I'm talking about was probably found more recently."

"Then go on back to the office and talk to some of the boss people involved in huntin' this stuff."

I had been trying to avoid that, not wanting to advertise my interest, especially since I'd been left with the impression that the chalice's ownership was in dispute. I didn't tell Marjorie that. I didn't have to; she read it in my face.

"Bud, you're workin' on some trouble again, aren't you?"

I nodded.

"Now you wait a minute. Let me take care of this gentleman."

I hadn't noticed anyone standing behind me. I stepped aside and let Marjorie ring up another sale. When she was finished, she said, "You know Captain Easy, don't you?"

"Jesus Estevez? I haven't seen him around in a few years."

"He's still here. Spends most of his time at home. Why don't you talk to him."

"Thanks, Marjorie, I'll do that."

"God bless, Bud."

I waved and left the museum. Jesus Estevez, more commonly known as Captain Easy, was a Cuban famous for his ability to free-dive to depths of twenty feet or more and stay down for two to three minutes at a time. Like Matt Johnson he had spent his life on the water, a lot of that time working for dive operators and the salvage industry; unlike Matt he wasn't a drunk. I wouldn't need a six-pack to get him to talk.

Before going to Captain Easy's, I stopped at home to call Ardis. I picked up the mail from the floor where it had been pushed through the slot in the door, then carried it over to the desk where I sat down and dialed Ardis's number.

"How's the patient?" I asked when she came on the line.

"Bud, there's nothing wrong with him."

"That's great news." I sorted through the mail. A couple of bills, the usual mix of junk mail, and a yellow slip from the post office notifying me they were holding a package for me. I put the slip in my pocket.

"He had a concussion," Ardis explained, her voice distant, "but they don't expect him to have any problems recovering from that. They want to keep him another day for observation."

"Wonderful. But you don't sound so happy. What's the problem?"

"Just. He seems so different."

"He'll come out of it."

"I'd hoped you would talk to him."

"Sure. I'll look in on him this evening."

After we hung up, I picked up the phone book and looked up Fred Pacey's number. I called and asked his secretary if I could speak to him. He was out of the office all day, she told me, her voice as cold as ice water. I asked about tomorrow. She took my name and suggested I call tomorrow.

I had better luck with the attorney Tim Kelly, who offered me an appointment at four o'clock. I looked at the clock on the wall behind me. It was past two. I got on my bike and rode over to Captain Easy's.

23

◇

Jesus Estevez lived on Petronia Street in a white clapboard shack that had recently been painted. A flowerbed was neatly arranged along the inside of the surrounding picket fence. The screen door was closed but not the front door, so I called out, "Jesus!"

A second later Estevez appeared, pushing open the screen door with his foot. He was trim, the size of a welterweight, a Cuban with skin the color of *café con leche.* His thick, black hair, combed straight back from his narrow forehead, glistened. It was impossible to determine his age, but I thought he was several years younger than I, in his early fifties maybe.

"It's Bud Lowry. I'd like to talk to you."

"Well, come on in. No reason to stand on the street, have all the neighbors hear your business."

I opened the gate and walked up the sidewalk. Estevez held the screen door open for me, motioned me inside. He had on an old-fashioned undershirt, which emphasized his muscular shoulders and chest.

The shack was one room with a kitchen and bath, the walls unfinished, the hardwood floors shiny. There were minimal furnishings but everything was clean and orderly. "You want a beer maybe?"

"I don't drink."

"A soda?"

"Nothing."

"Just talk."

"A couple of questions. I won't take much of your time."

"Time I got plenty of. I spend my days here now, taking care of this place, doing some woodwork. Time's not a problem."

"You don't dive anymore?"

He shook his head. "Been a couple of years since I last went down. Got a heart-valve problem, doc said give it up. Why mess with it, I say. It ain't no fun no more no way."

"Why not?"

"Like everything else, too damn many people and too much greed. Spend all their time in court fightin' each other and not enough in the water."

"That's what I want to talk about."

"Talk."

"I'm looking for a piece of treasure, an old wine chalice studded with stones. Emeralds, that kind of thing. You ever hear of it?"

Captain Easy flashed a smile. "Everybody's lookin' for treasure. They think you just get a boat, some divers, you go out and find the stuff like finding money somebody dropped on the street. Shit."

"What I'm talking about has already been salvaged. Now it's lost again."

Captain Easy nodded. "I heard of it."

"What do you know about it?"

"Come out here."

He went out the back door. I followed him across a small yard to a workshop that had been constructed along the back edge of his property. He opened the door, pulled the string on an overhead light. The shop smelled of wood shavings, machine oil, and the musty scent of mildewed leather. A long bench had racks for tools, and a band saw was in one corner. On the bench were model ships in various stages of completion. Extremely detailed, they looked as if they had been made to scale: a fleet of Spanish galleons, treasure ships much like those that had foundered on the reef surrounding the Keys in the seventeenth century.

"Here's where my time goes."

I moved over to the bench and examined the ships. They were quality craftsmanship; every spar and line and square-rigged canvas sailcloth looked picture-perfect. "Impressive. When did you start doing this?"

"Four, five years ago as a hobby. The last couple years, since I got the heart condition, it's been full-time."

"Modeled on actual ships?"

Captain Easy nodded. "Part of a fleet that left Havana harbor in 1621. Loaded with gold and silver from South America on their way back to Spain."

"You did the research on all this."

He laughed. "I got lucky. The treasure companies did that for me when they were trying to find the cargo manifest and trace the ships' route and where they wrecked. It took them years. All I did was read about it after. While everybody was looking for the gold, I decided to rebuild the fleet."

"You know what they were carrying?"

"Some of it. A lot of silver bars, gold coins. Indian

crafts. It was an annual journey, carrying the stuff back to Spain. The Spanish had been fighting a war over there for a lot of years and the government was about broke. They depended on that treasure coming in every year."

"That chalice I mentioned. Was something like that part of the cargo?"

"More likely belonged to one of the rich merchants who sometimes traveled with the cargo. Part of his personal tableware. Or could have been a special gift for King Philip."

"You said you'd heard of it. Any idea what happened to it, who found it?"

Captain Easy grinned. "Oh, sure. One outfit found it, another claims it was taken from their pile. It isn't like there's a goddamn bank down there in the ocean. After all these years, with storms and stuff, it had settled all over the place."

"But you know which ship it was on. Each outfit has claim over a ship, don't they?"

"True. But these guys are pirates, Bud. They find something from another ship, they ain't likely to give it back."

"What about the investors? They weren't pirates, were they?"

Captain Easy shrugged. "Some of 'em may have been. You know how it works, don't you, Bud? It took years to find some of these treasures. A lot of people went bust. And the ones who made it, a lot of times they didn't have money to put fuel in their boats. They sold shares. What do you call it? Speculating. You know, find people to put up money with a promise of part of the loot whenever it was found."

"High-risk speculating, I'd say."

"A couple of times it paid off."

"And a bunch of other times people lost their shirts."

"Probably. But so did Spain."

"Yeah, you've got a point. You ever hear of Joe Delgado and Brendan Scott?"

"Sure. I know Delgado. Scott's name rings a bell. I don't think I ever met him."

"Delgado claimed they found the chalice."

"Could be, I probably heard that. He got it now?"

I shook my head. Captain Easy grinned again. "You know, somethin' else besides treasure came over on these old ships."

"What was that?"

"Syphilis. Kind of makes me think they both are a lot alike."

"Gold and a virus. I guess they are. Back then they were both deadly."

Captain Easy smiled. "Too bad they haven't found a cure for gold."

24

◇

Tim Kelly's office on Whitehead Street was a short bike ride from Captain Easy's. I got there fifteen minutes early for my appointment. Water and sewer lines along here were being upgraded, while the street was being widened.

Standing on the front porch of Kelly's office, I watched as the heavy-equipment operators maneuvered their machinery through the layers of asphalt, brick, and soil, digging through the substratum. The air was thick with pulverized coral dust as the backhoes labored, trying to churn through the unyielding bedrock where murky gray water puddled. Beneath the surface our foundation was as harsh and unyielding as any, resistant to change.

Inside the office, the outside noise was only slightly muffled. "How do you stand it?" I asked the secretary.

She held up a pair of headphones attached to a CD player. "Sometimes it even gets through Bruce Springsteen." She smiled. "Do you have an appointment?" She was young and slender with an open, attractive face and thick auburn hair.

"At four. Gideon Lowry."

"I'll tell Tim you're here."

She stood up from her desk and, as discreetly as possible, tugged at her short skirt before sashaying down the hallway. A moment later she was back. "Just a minute and he'll be with you."

I sat down on one of the leather armchairs in front of a mahogany table where the usual assortment of waiting-room magazines was neatly stacked. The secretary donned her headphones after a darting, amused glance in my direction, then began typing at her computer. I watched her work. She was quickly absorbed, her lips parted slightly and the tip of her tongue curled over her lower lip.

"Mr. Lowry?"

I looked up. The lawyer had come up on my blind side. He was a young-looking forty-something with dark, curly hair, his shirtsleeves rolled up over muscular forearms. I stood up and offered my hand. "Gideon."

"Tim Kelly. Come on back to my office."

I followed him down the hallway and into the spacious office with its large desk in front of tiered shelves of law books. I sat down in a somewhat stiffer chair than the one in the front office while Kelly settled into the padded, high-backed one behind his desk.

"I knew your brother, Senator Lowry."

I nodded. Everyone had known Carl. Or thought they had. And they liked using his name, I'd noticed, now that he was dead, as if it were a sort of talisman that would establish a connection. "I've been hired to look into a matter involving the death of a young lady. Your name was mentioned in passing and I wondered if I could ask a couple of questions."

A frown creased Kelly's handsome features. "I suppose so. Can you tell me who gave you my name?"

"I'm afraid that's confidential."

Kelly adjusted the knot on his tie. "I understand. Who's the lady?"

"Katy Morgan."

A brief look of recognition crossed Kelly's face, I thought, before he recovered and stared blandly across the desk at me. "I think I read something about that."

"She worked for an escort service."

Kelly didn't say anything but his expression changed. He actually smiled.

"Your name was on the list of clients."

Now he laughed. "You're not running in any popularity contests, are you, Gideon?"

"It's the nature of my business. I sometimes have to dig into people's lives, and what I find there isn't always pretty. But you don't seem to be bothered."

"I'm not married and I haven't broken any laws that I know about."

"You were with her a lot?"

"Enough. There was something about her that kept you coming back."

I felt an irrational twinge of envy. "What was so special about Katy?

He laughed again. "In a word, sex. She was terrific."

"She ever talk about any problems she was having?"

"No. She knew how to focus. She was a pro. I mean that in the best sense of the word."

"What did you talk about, when you talked?"

"Me. She knew how to ask questions, to open a person up. I was careful not to talk about clients with her, but other than that she knew my life inside and out. In a way, I guess, it was a little bit like going to bed with your shrink. You never felt cheated with Katy, that's for sure."

"Ever aware of any interest she had in the treasure-salvage industry?"

Kelly looked thoughtfully up at the ceiling. "Not that I recall."

"She never talked about it."

"Well, we might have. I just don't remember."

"You represent some of the investors in that business, I understand."

Kelly looked at his watch. "I have." He was being evasive, like the other power brokers for whom Katy was just a nuisance.

"Any link that you know of between any one of them and Katy Morgan?" Like a drowning man I was reaching, trying to grasp on to any passing debris that might keep me afloat. But Kelly wasn't going to toss out any life jackets; instead he shook his head.

"I'm afraid I can't help you."

"And of course you wouldn't care to reveal those clients' names?"

He smiled. "Of course not."

I stood up. "If you think of anything, I'd appreciate a call."

We shook hands across the desk. I left his office. Someone else was in the waiting room. The secretary was still grooving on Bruce Springsteen and her word processor as I stepped out into the heat and the noise where the street digging had produced no more progress than my own excavation into Katy Morgan's past.

25

◇

A few minutes before five I remembered that I had a package at the post office. I biked quickly over to the red-brick building on Whitehead Street, built in the last decade but meant to pick up on the motif of the fortresses constructed around Key West during the Civil War.

A trio of kids on Rollerblades skated along the wide sidewalks leading up to the PO. I hurried up the steps, noticing the debris collected along the dirty tiles of the open-air exterior corridors. A postal clerk I knew was just locking the doors as I came up. I waved the yellow slip at him.

"Bud, your watch running slow these days?"

"No, just my memory. Can I pick this up?"

"Let me see it."

I handed him the yellow slip. He looked at it, grunted, then opened the door and disappeared inside. Most of my shopping was done by catalog, and I would frequently get packages whose contents I'd ordered some weeks earlier and forgotten. I assumed this was one of those occasions.

He returned moments later carrying a square box wrapped in brown paper. Nothing except my name and address was on the hand-printed label. According to the postmark it had been mailed Saturday. It had taken three business days for the receipt to get to me. U.S. postal efficiency! I cradled it under my arm, went back to my bike, put the box in the basket, and rode home.

It had been a long day. I was looking forward to a quiet evening when I remembered that Val's party was tonight, and I'd promised her that I would be there. I put the package on the desk. Nothing was on the answering machine. I flipped on the overhead fan and was about to sit down at the desk when I suddenly remembered that I had also promised Ardis I would look in on Just today. Was this forgetfulness the onset of old age? I wondered. I decided I'd better get out to see Just before it got any later.

The Buick was parked in the shade of a banyan tree along a side street, its interior relatively cool when I opened the door, rolled down the window, then got in and drove out to the hospital.

The judge was sitting up in bed watching the news on TV. When he saw me, he clicked the remote in his hand and the sound from the TV died.

"Bud, I was only just thinking about you."

"Ardis told me the news. Said everything's fine. You're going to get out of here tomorrow maybe."

Just nodded. He seemed distant, distracted. Not like a man who had recently been delivered from the possibility of a debilitating catastrophe.

"Bud, did Ardis say anything to you about Katy?" His voice was muffled, as though he didn't want anyone else to hear him, and he sounded depressed.

"No. She thought there was something going on that

you were keeping from her. I told her she would have to ask you about it. Did she?"

Just shifted in his bed. "It's all past history now, Bud. There's nothing any of us can do about it. Including you."

I couldn't ever remember hearing the judge sound quite so dismal.

"Well, maybe you're right, Just. But I'm working a couple of leads that might help explain why Katy took her life. I liked her and I'll do what I can for her. I think she would want that."

"Tell me what's going on."

I told him about my conversations with Captain Easy and Tim Kelly, as well as my unsuccessful effort to reach Fred Pacey.

"You're stepping on some pretty big feet, Bud."

"I'm also interested in looking through some of your court cases involving the treasure salvors. It's a long shot but one I think is worth the effort."

"What makes you think so?"

"Some background. These guys spend a lot of time in court. I'd like to know what they're fighting over."

"That sounds kind of slender, Bud. Especially if you're trying to connect it to Katy."

I hesitated. It wasn't like the judge to want to forestall an investigation. "I've also got a client now."

"Who's that?"

"Joe Delgado." I had mentioned Delgado before but without saying that I was working for him.

Just stared up at the silent TV screen. "You know about Delgado? He's been in and out of court on drunk-driving charges."

"That's what I'm getting at."

"What do you want me to do?"

"Ask your secretary to put together the necessary paperwork on cases for the past few years, as well as pending stuff. Let me go over them on the chance there's something there."

"I don't think there will be."

"I'd like to take a look at them anyway."

Just seemed to think about it for a while. "If you don't come up with anything, then what?"

"I don't know. I'll cross that bridge when I come to it."

"All right, I'll call her now and have her put the stuff together for you."

"Thanks. What about the marriage plans?"

"Ardis wants to go ahead with it once I'm released."

"What about you?"

"I'm having second thoughts."

"Any particular reason?"

Just lifted a hand. "Infirmity."

"I don't believe it."

"It creeps up on you. Sometimes it can swoop down until you wake up one morning like this."

I thought of my own earlier mental lapses. "Fight it."

Just nodded. "I will. But Ardis shouldn't have to."

26

◇

Val greeted me at the door of her apartment wearing a veil and a loose-flowing gown. Bells attached to her wrists and ankles jangled as she moved. She lifted the veil, her lips bright red, and kissed me on the mouth. "Gideon, honey, didn't I tell you it was a costume party? I must have forgotten."

As I stepped inside the apartment, the soft, complex tones of Eastern music drifted on the incense-scented air. Several couples swayed in a corner of the candlelit room; others sat on the floor sipping drinks, their conversation occasionally giving way to dark laughter. Everyone except me was masked, turbaned, or bejeweled. A woman passed by and tossed a feather boa around my neck, laughing as she pulled it free and moved on.

I followed Val to the bar where another veiled woman, this one wearing a halter top over pendulous breasts, mixed drinks. I asked for a club soda. Her dark eyes sparkled when she handed the drink to me.

"Now make yourself at home," Val said.

I was more ready to make *for* home.

"I know this isn't altogether social, so let Miss Val see if she can't find someone interesting for you to talk to."

When Val left, I huddled alone in a corner, watching the parade. Other than Val, I recognized no one, not even those people free of masks. Newcomers continued to pour in. Fifteen minutes after I had arrived the large room was filled and I was no longer able to find refuge in the corner. The music was drowned in a tangle of chatter; standing on the periphery of the party was like standing at the edge of madness. I thought.

Two guys in painted faces stopped and stared at me. One of them shrieked, "A foreigner!" The other took his hand and said, "Take me to the Casbah."

Desperately wanting a real drink, I found my way back to the bar and got a refill of soda. I noticed a sheen of sweat spread across the cleavage of the bartender.

Someone touched my shoulder as I tried to work my way out of the crowd. I turned and a woman wearing a black half-mask crooked a finger. I followed her. We wound through a stream of bodies, past a kitchen where people were eating, and down a hall.

My escort opened a door off the hallway and we started in before noticing the two painted guys clinging together, their hands groping at one another's crotch. They looked up and one of them said, "It's the foreigner."

"Maybe he's a spy," the other said.

"In the house of love." They giggled.

We backed out, closing the door, and moved down the hall where we found an empty room, a study, apparently Val's office. One window overlooked a lighted parking lot. My masked escort sat on the edge of a desk. The room was dark, the only illumination coming from the parking lot outside, filling the room with eerie shadows.

"Val said you wanted to know about Katy."

"Were you a friend of hers?"

"I suppose. We were roommates at one time. But Katy always kept her distance."

"Do you work for Val?"

She shook her head. "I have in the past, off and on. I got married six months ago."

"What's your name?"

"Paula."

"I'm Gideon." She offered her hand, which was cool and thin. I could feel her bones. "When was the last time you saw Katy?"

"We had lunch together a couple days before she died."

"How did she seem?"

"Burnt-out."

"Meaning?"

"She needed to get out of the business for a while. She was fried."

"Did she talk about it?"

"Well, she was saving money to go back to school, but she did talk about taking a vacation."

"Did she say where she was going?"

"No, she hadn't decided. She just needed to get off the rock for a while."

"Alone?"

"She didn't say."

"Did she mention any of her clients, any problems she might have been having?"

"There's always problems in this business."

"Anything specific, any person she was having trouble with?"

"No, not really. I got the feeling though that she had some problems."

"What kind of problems?"

"I'm not sure. Katy didn't talk much about herself. If it

155

hadn't been for what happened to her, I wouldn't have thought anything about it, but after she died I couldn't stop thinking about the last time I saw her and the things she said."

She reached up and pulled the mask up so that it perched on the top of her head. The muted light from the parking lot fell on a face as smooth and unblemished and nearly as translucent as an empty eggshell. Her eyes were hard to read. She might have been lying; she might have been telling the truth. She could do either, I thought, with the same bland expression. But she had no apparent reason to lie to me. "What do you remember about that conversation?"

"She mentioned that she was trying to sell something, which was what gave me the idea she might have been having financial problems."

"Selling what?"

"Katy didn't say exactly, just that it was an heirloom, which is how I got the idea that it was worth some money."

"Did she say she had a buyer, or anyone interested?"

Paula thought for a moment. Her tongue darted out, moistening her lips. "I'm not sure. I think so, but I don't really remember."

"Did she mention any names?"

"No. It was really just in passing. Like I said, I wouldn't have thought any more about it if she hadn't died the way she did."

"Did she ever talk to you about her family? Or how she might have come across a valuable heirloom?"

Paula shook her head. "She was born in Key West, but I think she moved around a lot when she was growing up. Her mother's dead and I don't think she knew her father."

That squared with what Katy had told me. The door opened and Val looked in. "I was wondering where you two had disappeared. Why are you in the dark? Are you learning anything, Gideon?"

"Paula's been a big help."

Paula's expression didn't change. "I don't know. I wish I could be of more help. Katy was really sweet and probably too tender to be in this business."

I looked at Val, who had said the same thing, although she recognized that Katy's fragility had been an enhancement.

"Do you think the police are going to want to talk to me?" Paula asked.

I shrugged. "I doubt that they're pursuing this now."

"Well, unless there's anything else, I'll get back to the party."

"Sure. Thanks for what you've told me."

"I wish I knew more." Paula went out. Val closed the door behind her.

"Paula's one of the lucky ones."

"How so?"

"She married a client, a doctor."

"Too bad that didn't happen to Katy."

"I don't think Katy was looking for that kind of life. Despite her emotional intensity, she was pretty independent."

"Or scared of having her parents' life repeated."

"Was Paula really helpful?"

"I think so." I knew, of course, that I was just dancing in the dark in search of a clue, something that would put me on track, something Katy could have provided, but she was dead. The next best thing was to get to the people who knew her best. Except that no one seemed to know her at all.

I said good-night to Val, who slipped her hand in mine and led me through the crowd to the door, kissing me on the lips before I went out.

On the chance I might see Pepper, I drove down to the club and took the elevator to the top floor. I was lucky. He was sitting at the bar talking to Ronnie, and the place was nearly empty. Smiling at Ronnie, I sat down on the barstool next to Pepper.

"Gideon, welcome. Ronnie told me you were in the other night warming up."

"That's why I came by. We still on for the weekend?"

"By all means, of course, Gideon. Don't let these midevening doldrums fool you. By midnight the joint will jump."

Ronnie put a club soda in front of me.

Like me, Pepper was a conch. A decade or so younger than I, he had worked most of his life in the bar business, managing one club or another. Some years ago he had made his peace with the direction Key West had decided to take and had followed it with a sure sense of the various cycles of cultural fashion, always seeming to have just the right entertainment lined up for whatever was current. My particular style had been in vogue for a few years now, but I was always waiting for the hammer to fall.

"I heard about the judge's accident," Pepper said. "How is he?"

"He's going to make it."

Pepper shook his head. "I'm glad to hear that. I heard he'd had a drink or two that night."

I nodded. "He was giving a party and ran out of ice. He went out to get some and was on his way back when it happened."

Pepper smiled. "Ironic, isn't it. The judge is a good guy, but he's always been a little harsh when it comes to sentencing drivers who were drinking."

I remembered that Peggy had mentioned the same thing earlier in the day. It was ironic, a fact that would certainly not have been lost on the judge. Which reminded me that I was supposed to pick up the appearances on his court calendar tomorrow.

"Thanks, Pepper."

"For what?"

"Reminding me of something I need to do." I drank my soda.

Pepper grinned. "Whatever that might have been."

On the ride home I kept having flashbacks of the party at Val's, of the emotionless woman who had told me about Katy in Val's darkened office. It had been a bizarre evening. Then I thought about Patrick and the ride up the Keys the other night, the effect it might have had on him. And I thought how all of this had started the morning the judge asked me to meet him for breakfast and I found out he was planning to get married. Had it not been for that decision, none of this would be happening.

Or would it? There was still Katy Morgan's suicide hanging in the balance.

I parked the Buick and came in the back way. Tom was on the porch. He stood up and stretched, following me inside. I found a couple of leftover cooked shrimp and gave them to him.

Then I sat down at my desk in the office. The parcel I had picked up from the post office earlier was on the desk. I read the hand-printed label again, noting the lack of a return address. With a letter opener, I broke through the tape sealing the paper. Inside the wrapping was an ordinary, unmarked cardboard box that had been used more than once, with more tape sealing its flaps. I cut through the tape and opened it. I thought I knew what the cloth-wrapped object was even before I touched it. I wasn't wrong. Pulling the cloth away, I put the gold wine chalice on the desk in front of me and turned it, watching the emeralds glint as they caught the dim light from the desk lamp.

For quarter of an hour maybe, I sat there staring, transfixed by this four-hundred-year-old piece of treasure that men had died for, and now I was more than certain that it had been a factor in Katy's death. She had wanted me to have it, to protect it for her until she could do something with it, make some decision. The decision she made being a final one.

At last I stood up, put the chalice back in the box and carried it to my bedroom and knelt down in front of the small safe I kept there, ran through the numbers of the combination, and sealed the chalice inside.

I couldn't get to sleep for a long time, and when sleep finally came, I dreamed that I was alone in a car, driving along an empty asphalt road that stretched away into infinity. The car had a volition of its own, traveling faster and faster along the smooth road. I knew I had no control over it and that eventually the road was going to end.

Just as I was hurtling toward a dark abyss at the end of the road, I woke up. The first light of day slanted across the bed and my body was soaked in sweat.

◇

After that I drifted in and out of sleep, unwilling perhaps to face another day like the previous one when nothing seemed to add up. Lying in bed in that dreamy state reminded me of my drinking days when I'd wake before dawn and ease into the grayness of day fighting a fierce hangover. It had been bittersweet, waiting for the edge to wear off while still lurking in that whiskey-induced subterranean dream world.

At eight o'clock I finally got up, slipped into a pair of khakis and a T-shirt, and went across to the *grocería* and got a coffee and some toasted Cuban bread with cheese, which I carried back and ate before reluctantly opening up shop.

I had showered and was scraping my face with a razor when I heard the bells clang over the door in the office. "Be right there," I called, and, after rinsing my face and pulling on the T-shirt, walked barefoot into the front room. Ardis was seated in the chair in front of my desk.

161

It was five minutes past nine by the pendulum clock behind the desk. I sat down. I pushed aside the crumpled wrapping paper from the night before.

"A present?"

"In a manner of speaking. Is everything all right? The judge is—"

Ardis smiled. "Everything's fine. He comes home this morning and I'm getting an early start doing some shopping. I wanted to come by and thank you."

"For what?"

"For what you did for Patrick. I don't know what you said to him the other night, but whatever it was, it worked. He's changed."

"What do you mean?"

"He wants to stay here and help me with Just."

"You're kidding." I wondered how this news would affect the judge.

Ardis shook her head. "I owe you my thanks. I know I should have dealt with him some time ago. I let things go too long. But sometimes it's easier for someone outside the family to influence a boy that age."

"I can't take any credit for him. He's probably not so bad anyway by today's standards. What's he going to do?"

"I'd like for him to get a job. I think it might be good for him. Once he gets through the summer, maybe he'll have a better idea what he wants to do."

"What kind of a job?"

"I was hoping you might help him."

"What can he do?"

"Anything if he sets his mind to it. He's just like his mother." Ardis laughed.

An idea hit me. I leaned back in the chair and thought about it for a moment. "Let me make a call. Would he be willing to work as an apprentice for experience but not much money?"

"What is it?"

I reached for the phone book and looked up a number, then picked up the phone and dialed. I got a beeper and punched in my own number and hung up.

"A job on a boat," I told Ardis.

"That sounds interesting. What kind of a boat?"

"A treasure-hunting boat."

Ardis looked perplexed. "But I don't know what Patrick could do."

"Change fuel filters. And if he's lucky, learn some other skills in the process."

"Well—"

The phone rang. I picked it up.

"Joe Delgado here."

"Joe, it's Gideon. I may have solved a small problem for you."

"What's that?"

"I've got a kid who's willing to do some of that donkey work you were moaning about." I winked at Ardis. "He doesn't have a lot of experience, but he'll work through the summer for low wages and whatever he can learn."

"I don't know—"

"You'd be doing me a favor if you would give him a shot at it."

Delgado hesitated. "What's his name?"

"Patrick Whelan."

"All right. Tell him to show up at the boat at eight tomorrow morning, but I can't make any promises."

"None expected." I thanked him and hung up. "Patrick's got a shot at a job," I told Ardis. "Eight o'clock tomorrow morning down at the dock at the foot of Grinnell Street."

Ardis stood up. "That's wonderful, Gideon. You know how to get things done." She smiled. "And don't worry about the judge. He'll be in good hands." She walked to the door, turning to smile and wave as she went out.

Once she was gone, I sat at the desk for a while, wondering about Ardis Whelan, the way in which she could transform herself from nervous uncertainty one moment to a kind of carefree giddiness the next.

Shortly after ten, I went down to the courthouse. Judge Watson's secretary, a woman in her midforties who had been with the judge for a couple of decades, was at her desk. "Morning, Ms. Albury."

"How are you, Mr. Lowry?" In the years I had stopped by here to see the judge—and they were many—we had never referred to one another in any other way. I might have invited her to call me Gideon, but she insisted on the formality. I had asked the judge about it once, and he said that was the way she saw her job, everyone got treated equally, without any outward sign of partiality.

Ms. Albury had on a pleated skirt with a patterned blouse and a scarf tied tightly at her neck. She wore utilitarian glasses. Her thick hair, worn short, was beginning to turn gray. The only adornment was a vase of freshly cut flowers on her desk.

"The judge gets out of the hospital this morning," I said. "Have you heard from him?"

"He called me yesterday."

I nodded. "Did he happen to mention I might be stopping in for his court calendar?"

"He did. I've got it right here." Ms. Albury opened a drawer and took out a file folder, which she handed me.

"Thanks." I leafed through the pages and saw that it contained only the upcoming calendar. The judge must have forgotten that I had wanted to see the old stuff, too. "I wonder how much trouble it would be to dig up some old records of the trials the judge presided over."

"How far back would you like to have them?"

"Oh, I don't know. Say, ten years. Is that out of the question?"

"Ms. Albury smiled. "Not at all. How detailed would you like the information, Mr. Lowry?"

"Names, dates, convictions, and sentences would be sufficient. If it isn't too much trouble."

The same brief smile played across her thin lips. "It might take some time."

"At your convenience, of course."

"I understand. I'll try to have something for you before the end of the day."

I wanted to hug her. Instead, I said, "Thank you, Ms. Albury. I'll stop back then."

Back home I went through the file she had given me. Of course Joe Delgado's name was there, but none of the other names meant anything to me. I had hoped that by digging into some of the past cases we might find a link to the present. It was a long shot, but those were all the shots I seemed to have right now.

28

◇

The judge looked wan, somewhat shrunken, his hair spiky with neglect. Giving me a sad smile, he lifted his large hands from his lap. "Well, here I am," he said.

"Which is better than where you could be right now," Ardis replied, "unless you believe in heaven and think that you had a chance of getting in there."

We were in the judge's study, where Just insisted he wanted to be when he came home. Ardis had tidied it up and put some fresh flowers around the room. I had asked her how he was doing when I came to the house, and all Ardis would say was, "Grumpy."

She had on the same pair of shorts and matching shirt outfit she had been wearing when she came by my place earlier in the morning. She had put the usual effort into her appearance, but she looked tired, as if she hadn't slept much the past couple of nights.

"Bud, I'm glad you came by," Just said, "Ardis, would you let me talk to him for a minute?"

Ardis looked hurt but didn't say anything. She turned and left the room. "Close the door, Bud," Just said.

I stepped over and closed the door to the study, then went and sat down on the couch opposite Just's desk. "I picked up those papers from Ms. Albury this morning," I said.

"Find anything useful in them?"

"Not so far."

"Want to tell me what your hunch was, why you wanted that information?"

"Some of these treasure hunters have spent as much time in court as they have in the water. There've been legal battles between salvage companies and even infighting within companies. Katy knew these guys. She was involved with them. I'd hoped one of those cases might shed some light on that wine chalice I told you about, and since you've presided over most of them, it seemed only prudent to check your records."

"Where do you go now?"

"I'm not sure. It's gotten more complicated." I told him about receiving the chalice in the mail.

The judge looked astounded. "Who the hell do you think sent it to you?"

"Katy Morgan. She even mentioned that maybe I should hold it for her when she told me about it on Saturday. I didn't think she was serious. Apparently, she was. She must have mailed it to me that same day."

"Why?"

"She was scared for some reason and decided the safest thing she could do would be to mail it to me."

"Why do you think she didn't put her name on it?"

"I don't know. Maybe it was an oversight. Maybe she was so damned scared that she didn't want any connection with it once she decided to send it to me."

Just nodded. "Do you have any hunches on this one,

Bud? Anything that might explain why she killed herself?"

"When she told me about that chalice, she was scared but she didn't seem depressed. She was thinking about her life, her future. Something happened in twenty-four hours to change that. I don't think the chalice had anything directly to do with her death."

"What else?"

I shook my head. "To Katy it was just a piece of gold, something that could help turn her life around, give her a head start. Whatever claim she thought she might have had to it was nullified by the terrible news she got, something so horrible she couldn't face it. I think she must have known, just by having sent it to me, that, after her death, I would face it for her."

"What about the police?"

"As far as I know, their investigation is stalled."

Just stared out the bay window that looked over the side yard. "I wish I could be of help, Bud."

We sat in silence for a moment.

"Well, Bud, I guess there's something you should know."

I thought Just was going to tell me something about Katy Morgan, but instead he surprised me by saying he wasn't going to marry Ardis. He made his announcement in a hushed voice and then sat there at his desk with his hair sticking up and a sour look on his face.

"Have you told her yet?"

"No, I haven't."

"What made you change your mind?"

He tried to smile but it quickly disappeared. "Old mortality has knocked once. I guess that's enough."

"I told you the other day, you've got years left. Something like this happens and you beat it, it only makes you stronger."

Just shook his head. "I'm an old man. She's too young to be saddled with me."

"Shouldn't she be the one to make that judgment?"

"I can't do it."

"Is that all there is to it, the difference in your ages?"

Just looked at me suspiciously. "What else?"

"I don't know. I was wondering, that's all."

He didn't say anything.

"You know Patrick's decided to stay here. I got him a job on Joe Delgado's boat."

"When did this happen?"

"This morning."

"Ardis asked you?"

"She came by. She told me Patrick's attitude has changed."

"I wonder what changed it." Just looked at me with the same look of suspicion.

"I don't know. Ardis insists he's not a bad kid, just a little confused right now. I think Patrick feels bad about that accident. Especially happening after you had that argument."

"What argument?"

"Before you went to get the ice. You don't remember?"

Just seemed to think about it. "I don't remember much before the accident. What was the argument about?"

"I was leaving the party. I was coming out to say good-night when I overheard the two of you. You'd asked Patrick to go and get the ice. He objected."

Just nodded. "That sounds vaguely familiar."

"It isn't Patrick that's causing you to back down, is it?"

"No, Bud, it isn't Patrick."

"Well, all right. I wanted to make sure."

We sat silently for a minute staring out the window.

"You may not know it, Bud, but over the years I've

made some investments which have brought me some money."

"I assumed you were comfortable."

"More than comfortable. You're the closest family I've got. I want you to handle my estate when I die."

I felt uncomfortable. "I wish you'd stop talking about dying." It was distressing to watch him. He seemed like a man who had accepted some fate that only he was aware of. "You've got plenty of life left in you."

The judge shrugged. "Maybe. And maybe not. I want my house to be in order, that's all. Have we got anything else to talk about? I'm beginning to tire."

"I don't think so. I'll look in on you tomorrow."

The judge sat in his chair, his eyes closed, and said, "Thanks, Bud, you've been a good friend."

It had a sound of finality that I didn't like. I went out and closed the door.

◇

Ardis's retreating back was visible down the hallway as I left Just's study. I had the feeling that she might have been outside the study door, listening. I found her in the kitchen removing things from the refrigerator. She was bent over pulling food out and slamming it down on the counter. When she closed the door and saw me, she said, "Do you know that he has eaten the same thing for lunch every day for most of his life?"

"I never paid any attention." Or maybe I hadn't eaten lunch with him that often.

"A sandwich. Roast beef one day, ham and cheese the next. Every day for years." She sounded angry.

"You're going to change that?" I didn't recognize any of the items she had hauled from the fridge.

"I'm going to try. You'd think someone as skilled in the kitchen as he is would vary his eating habits, wouldn't you?"

"Well, if he likes it—"

Ardis waved her hand in dismissal. "All that white bread. I may not cook, but I know what's good for him."

She was spreading a thick, yellowish paste on thin triangles of some kind of unleavened bread. "What's that?"

"Hummus." She had her back to me, her head bowed as she worked, something stiff and tense about her movements. "It's made with chickpeas, olive or sesame oil, and garlic. I discovered it years ago when we were living in the Middle East. It's good. Want some?" Without looking at me, Ardis pushed one of the triangles off to the side. "It's on pita bread."

I declined. A roast beef sandwich sounded pretty good, I thought. I wasn't sure Just was ready for this, wherever it came from, but I didn't say anything to Ardis.

I stood leaning against the counter while she fussed with the food. "I don't know why I'm doing this," Ardis suddenly said. She flung the knife, sending it clattering into the sink. I stepped away from the counter.

"Ardis?"

"I don't have to go through this, you know." She turned toward me, her eyes red-rimmed.

"I know you don't." I wondered how much she had heard.

"He can take care of himself, live the rest of his life in that damned study if he wants to." She stood with one hand on her hip, the other clenched tightly in a fist on the counter.

I didn't say anything.

"I can go back to my place until he comes to his senses." Ardis looked away from me.

"Maybe he needs a little time," I said lamely.

She looked back at me, a strange smile on her face. "He's had all his life. I was foolish to believe he was going to change now."

"He's been through a lot."

"So have I." Ardis began putting things back in the refrigerator, cleaning up. "The next time you talk to him, have one of your boy talks, tell him I've gone home. When he wants me, he knows how to use the phone."

I said it might be a good idea for her to talk to him. She turned back to me, a hint of moisture in her eyes. "I've tried. I've tried."

By the time I got downtown I was fifteen minutes late for the appointment I had finally been able to get with Fred Pacey.

Pacey was not a local, but he'd been in the Keys for years, a man who had no doubt broken bread with my brother, Carl, the late state senator, and who only knew me through him. His office was located on the second floor of a three-story, red-brick building overlooking the waterfront. The building had been renovated several years ago and had an open stairway up through the atrium, in the center of which an interior fountain gushed aggressively. Palm trees in large clay pots were dotted around the terrazzo floor, and various shops opened onto the atrium, no doubt part of Pacey, Inc.

In the outer office where I announced myself to Pacey's secretary, a row of framed posters depicting old landmark Key West buildings were along one wall, the buildings themselves now gone or gussied up beyond recognition. Pacey's secretary made a show of looking at her watch, then back at me as if I were something the dog had dragged home. "It'll be a few minutes," she said pointedly, "Mr. Pacey's on the phone." She pronounced his name with reverence.

Keeping plenty of distance between us, I studied the pictures on the walls. It was interesting, I reflected, that for the most part what Pacey was selling no longer existed, largely due to his efforts to remove anything funky in order to make Key West sufficiently homogeneous for the type of tourist he liked to see here; namely, people who came in for a day or two and did not want to see anything derelict or down-at-the-heels, people who liked their quaintness to be photographed and framed, something they could purchase in a gift shop. A Pacey gift shop.

Ten minutes later, a buzzer sounded and the secretary told me I could go in. I opened the door into Pacey's inner sanctum and found him seated behind a huge desk in front of a long plate-glass window that framed a cruise ship tied to the dock barely two hundred yards away.

Fred looked chipper. For a moment I felt a twinge of regret, knowing I was going to change his mood. He stood up, tucking his white shirt into his suit pants, and offered his hand across the expanse of highly polished walnut desk. Pacey was fair-haired with baby-soft skin and features to match. I had no idea how old he was, but I did know, from pictures that had appeared in the local paper's society pages, that Pacey had a family. There was something callow and half-grown about him, and I had a hard time picturing Pacey with Katy Morgan. He seemed asexual, almost prepubescent.

"Gideon, I don't think I've seen you since your brother's death."

That was a few years ago. Our paths really never crossed.

Pacey motioned for me to sit down in one of the twin leather armchairs in front of his desk. He made a show of looking at his watch, a thin gold band on his wrist, and sat back down. A busy man with an empty desk.

"Now what was it you wanted to talk about?"

"I'm working on a case. It involves the death of a young lady."

"Oh, who is that?"

"Katy Morgan. She worked for Valentine's, an escort service."

There was a hesitation before Pacey tried to cover it with a forced laugh, but his expression had changed, as I knew it would. He now looked grim. "Why the hell would you be asking me about that, Gideon? I didn't know Katy Morgan."

"You used Val's services, didn't you?"

"Who told you that?" Pacey managed to get a slight edge of menace in his voice.

"What's the difference, it's a fact. There's been a death and I'm investigating it."

"Who hired you?"

"Come on, Fred. You know that's confidential. Help me out here."

The hesitation was longer this time, with no attempt to cover it by nervous laughter. "Sorry, Gideon, I've got nothing to say. I believe the police investigated that girl's death and it was ruled a suicide."

"That's right. Did they question you?" Clearly, I had gotten under his skin. Therefore, it seemed unlikely that the police had pressed him too closely about Katy. She was dead and buried now, and he must have hoped that his secret life with her was buried, too.

Pacey squirmed, shifting in his comfortable chair. "They did, and they were satisfied."

"With what?"

"That I couldn't be of any help to them."

"Maybe they didn't ask the right questions."

"As far as I'm concerned, it's a dead issue."

A wisp of charcoal smoke belched from the stacks on the cruise ship. I sat there silently watching it spiral skyward, thinning into the atmosphere.

"Who gave you my name?"

I shook my head again. Pacey stood up, turning his

back to me, and looked out at the ship. Line handlers were releasing lines as the ship prepared to get under way.

"Your brother, Carl, was a friend of mine." Pacey continued to stare out the window.

"I assumed he was."

"It seems to me you were involved in a case just before he died, one that caused some embarrassment for innocent people."

"That's the nature of my business."

Pacey turned to face me, gripping the back of his chair. "You're not going to do that to me."

I didn't say anything.

"Because if you do, I'll hold you accountable. If this story leaks out in any way, I'll hold you personally responsible." Fred Pacey's interests were money and image. The message he was delivering was that nothing was going to interfere with his acquisition of either.

"I want answers to a couple of questions. That's all."

"I knew Katy Morgan. But I don't know anything about her death. Period."

I smiled. "I wasn't accusing you of anything."

"There's nothing I can add to what I've told the police, Gideon."

"Did she ever hit you up for money?"

Pacey shook his head.

"Never tried to sell you anything?"

He shoved his hands in his pockets. "Yeah, she tried to sell me something."

"What?"

"She never said. She called me one day and said she had a valuable piece of treasure, something from Key West's history."

"Did she show it to you?"

"No. She never got around to it. She called only a couple of days before she died."

The cruise ship spewed a thicker cloud of smoke; its horn shattered the stillness as it began to ease away from the dock, making its escape.

Pacey looked at his watch again. A buzzer sounded and he picked up the phone. He put his hand over the mouthpiece. "I have another appointment. I've told you everything I know."

I stood up. He didn't offer his hand, and I made my escape.

30

◇

Other than disrupting Fred Pacey's placid existence, I seemed to have achieved little except to confirm that Katy associated with influential clients, Key West's business establishment. Par for the course with this investigation, I thought. Hitting up against brick walls every turn I took.

Discouraged, I stopped by Yesterday's and found Webb Conners behind a hot roast-beef sandwich plate piled high with mashed potatoes. "Sit, Bud, sit," Webb said. I sat down in the booth opposite him.

"How's the hawkshaw business today, Bud?" Webb had always been amused that I'd become a private detective, and he never missed an opportunity to amuse himself more by coming up with some old-fashioned monikers like *hawkshaw* and *gumshoe.*

"I just came from talking to Fred Pacey."

"Oh, what kind of trouble's he in?"

A waitress came by and took my order. A roast beef

sandwich on rye. I thought of Ardis and her hummus.

"He was mixed up with Katy Morgan."

"You don't say. Pacey? I never figured him to be into that."

"Some would probably have said the same about you, Webb."

He ducked his head as some color spread over his face. When he looked up, his expression was more serious. "You're still pursuing that, are you, Bud? You got any leads?"

"I'm working a couple of different angles."

"I guess Eberhardt's investigation has stalled."

"I don't know. I haven't talked to Bill recently. I don't know what's going on there."

"How's the judge?" Changing the subject seemed to help Webb relax somewhat.

"He's out of the hospital. He's going to be okay."

"Still getting married?"

"As far as I know." Webb Conners belonged to the courthouse crowd where gossip was currency. Out of respect for the judge I wasn't about to pay into it.

"What do you know about her, Bud?"

"Who?"

"The judge's fiancée."

"Ardis Whelan." Neither was I going to betray my feelings about Ardis for courthouse fodder. "She seems okay."

"People are talking about her."

"I'm sure they are. That's what people do in this town."

"Well, they think maybe she's moved in on him a little too fast."

I laughed. "My God, Webb, the judge is pushing seventy and no one's moved in on him in fifty years. What makes you think he's going to start being taken in now? Next you'll tell me she's an outsider."

"Don't think that hasn't been mentioned."

Of course I had to remember my own early suspicions when the judge first told me he was getting married. It's just the way we thought down here. "Just can take care of himself," I said. And the truth was it looked as if he was going to have to.

Webb finished his lunch just as the waitress brought my sandwich. He ordered a piece of Key lime pie and coffee. "Just to keep you company," Webb said, smiling.

I took a bite out of the sandwich. "Is Pacey involved with any of the treasure outfits?"

"I heard he had some money tied up in them. Why?"

"Katy was working an angle of her own there. I got a little present in the mail yesterday."

"That's your lead?" The waitress arrived with his pie and coffee.

"Katy was looking for money."

"So she was hitting on guys like Pacey?"

I nodded. "She had something to sell."

"She sure did." Webb grinned, some pie filling stuck to his lip.

"She ever hit you up?"

"You kidding? She was going after the money crunchers. Why would she bother with me?"

A good question, I thought, finishing my sandwich before Webb did his pie. "I'll see you around." I left some money on the table.

"Don't take any plug nickels."

It was the common parting remark of our youth. I nodded and left, feeling a sense of sadness.

31

◇

From a pay phone outside Yesterday's I called Ms. Albury, who surprised me when she told me that the list of the judge's previous court cases that I had asked for was ready. I walked around to her office and picked it up, then went home and spent a good part of the afternoon going over the lists, back through years of courtroom documents.

It was time-consuming work, reading through the names, the court cases, the sentences handed down. Although some of the defendants were familiar, most of them local people, it was surprising how many I'd never heard of. I checked names from this list against those I had gotten from Val. After a couple hours I'd gotten nowhere.

I checked off half a dozen names I thought merited closer scrutiny, but I was barely a quarter of the way through the total list when the front door opened and Bill Eberhardt came in. "Bud," he said, then took out a handkerchief and stood in the middle of the floor, mopping his forehead. His shirt was sweat-stained; he looked hot and uncomfortable and his demeanor suggested that he wasn't in such a good mood.

"Pull the chair up under the fan. You'll cool down."

Bill lumbered over, glancing up at the fan, and positioned the chair.

"This is April. Think what the summer's going to be like. It's getting hotter every year. Does it seem that way to you, Bud?"

I shrugged. Every year it was the same, the brief cooler temperatures of winter, then on the first hotter than usual spring day, people began to anticipate the summer with dread.

"How long have you lived here?"

"Twenty years. Why?"

"Time you got used to the climate."

"Bud, some things you never get used to. For me, heat's one of them. Another is being lied to."

"Who lied to you?"

"You did."

"I don't think so."

"You didn't tell me about Delgado."

"So?"

"He was seen with Katy Morgan the night before she died. They had an argument. You were a witness to that argument."

"So? I thought you'd closed the book on this one. Katy killed herself. You told me that yourself. Why you bothering about an argument she had with Delgado?"

"Something troubles me about this case, Bud. Something in the back of my mind keeps telling me there's more to this than depression and suicide. And the fact that you're still involved tells me I'm right."

"Where'd you hear that?"

"Word gets around."

"Delgado's my client. Which is why I didn't mention him. And that's not lying. It's just good business policy."

"It has to do with that wine cup, doesn't it. Delgado was after it and he thought Katy Morgan had it. But it wasn't in that trailer. At least not when we looked through her things." Eberhardt looked at me suspiciously. "After you'd already been in there."

I just looked at him, without speaking.

"You know where it is, Bud?"

"Maybe I do."

"You know it's evidence. It's got to be turned over to the police. You could go to jail over this."

"Evidence of what? You've as much as admitted that there's been no crime here."

"And you told me that cup didn't belong to Katy."

"And now she's dead."

"You said you knew where it was."

"I said maybe."

"Either you do or you don't."

"Black-and-white, is it?"

Eberhardt pushed two fingers between his thick neck and his shirt collar, moving his head back and forth. When he had loosened his collar, he said, "Where is it, Bud?"

"As soon as I know for sure, I'll tell you."

From his expression I could see that he thought I was lying. But I was sure he wasn't going to press it, not right now anyway.

"You're getting people's backs up."

"Am I? I guess that happens when you're in the line of business we're in."

"You're stepping on toes."

"I've already been reminded of that. But they happen to be the same toes you've already stepped on."

"You know what I mean, Bud."

"Yeah, I know exactly what you mean. These people with their backs up don't want their names dragged into this. You've been able to protect them. They're not sure they can get the same treatment from me."

"Now, Bud."

"Don't now-Bud-me, Bill. You know exactly what I'm talking about. Fred Pacey. Tim Kelly. Maybe others who I haven't even gotten to yet. The word is out. Gideon Lowry's on the loose. So you've been called on to slow me down. Isn't that it, Bill? Isn't that what this little visit's really about?"

"Keep your cool, Bud."

"You're the one who came in here all hot and bothered."

Eberhardt stood up. "Let me know—when you know, that is—where it is."

"You'll be the first, Bill. Now stay out of the sun."

32

◇

Damn it. My hand began to tremble just slightly beneath the desk. I laughed; it came out sounding like a bark. I had turned the tables on Bill Eberhardt, all the while knowing that I was on the verge of falling; skating on thin ice as they said. I couldn't keep this up. Sooner or later he would be forced to pull me in for questioning, if for no other reason than harassing private citizens. But for the time being, at least, I thought we were still friends.

After Eberhardt had gone I sat back in the chair and tried to relax. I thought of Katy Morgan, the night we had stood in this very room, half-naked, the smell of her hair, our bodies. She had asked me about the photos of my mother and father, confessing that she had only recently come to know her own father. It was a moment, just a moment, when I remembered feeling that Katy had something more she wanted to tell me, something she was holding back, just as she had tried to hold back the tears that welled in her eyes when she looked up at me. I sent her home in a taxi, and though I never expected to see her again, Katy had struck a chord in me, one that I had not heard since Casey's departure.

Then, I remembered that it was Casey who had driven me to Katy in the first place. Casey with her call from Miami to tell me she was getting married.

I reached for the phone.

"Bud? What a surprise. Is everything all right?" Casey's voice was bright, cheery.

"Just feeling a little defeated. You got a minute?"

"Of course. I'm working at home doing some graphics for Mike."

"Still getting married next month?"

Casey laughed. "Yes. Neither of us has gotten cold feet yet. Why, did you think we would?"

"Your announcement came on the heels of another one—"

"Judge Watson's. I remember."

"His is off. I thought I'd check with you."

"You think these things run in pairs? Bud, what's going on? You sound low."

I told her. Back to that initial breakfast I'd had with Just and my encounter with Katy, right up to the present. I described in detail the various incidents and stumbling blocks in my effort to find out why Katy had killed herself, including Just's mysterious behavior and Ardis's departure. I told her about the wine chalice and the people I'd talked to.

Casey seemed fascinated by Captain Easy and saddened by Matt Johnson, whom she knew from AA on the occasional times when he had attended meetings in an effort to get sober.

When I finished, for no apparent reason I felt better. Casey was uninvolved and I could talk to her about it in a way that I couldn't with anyone here. Also, I had to admit, it felt good just talking to Casey again.

Then she surprised me. "I don't know if it will be any help, but I can tell you a little about Brendan Scott."

"You know him?"

"I don't, but Mike does. Bud, don't you remember? I told you we'd done some advertising work for him. The boat races in Key West. Remember?"

Oh, yes. Another slip. I could make excuses: other things had gotten in the way, crowding out distant information that seemed at the time to be of little importance. But the fact was, my memory was going. The short-term stuff that everyone talked about as being the product of old age. I had no trouble recalling with too vivid clarity events from the past, but apparently holding on to a conversation from yesterday or last week was like holding rainwater in a sieve.

"I remember," I said, somewhat vaguely.

"Well, Scott is a honcho in the powerboat races, one of the members of the committee that organizes the races in south Florida. He's got connections in various schemes to turn a fast profit. He's been involved in treasure hunting for a number of years with limited success, but apparently his real ability is getting people to invest in his schemes."

It came back to me now. Casey had told me about Delgado having some legal problems and that he was going before the judge. She had also been the first to link Delgado to Scott.

"What made you dig this up?"

After a brief silence at the other end, Casey said, "Oh, I don't know. I had a hunch you might be interested."

"You're right. Thanks."

"Bud, you're sure that everything's okay?"

"Yeah. I'm not drinking, but I find myself having mental lapses now and then."

I could sense Casey's relief. "Of course you are, Bud. It goes with the territory of getting sober. It takes time. Don't worry about it."

"I'm in a business where I have to worry about it."

"Those brain cells will regenerate. In the meantime start taking notes."

"Thanks for not reminding me that I'm getting old. What else did you find out about Scott? Anything personal?"

"As a matter of fact, yes. He's been married three times, his first wife died, and the last one's collecting alimony. He's a gambler, a hustler, perhaps there've been some shady deals along the way, but he's had no direct conflict with the law that I know of. He plays his cards close to his chest. He drinks. He takes up with strippers and hookers. I suppose he's found that it's cheaper than alimony. Since the last wife, no long-term relationships."

"I'm impressed. How'd you find this out?"

"Mike did. Over a beer with Scott."

"Mike drinks?"

"Not on your life. He had a Coke. Scott had the beer. Mike's just good at getting people to open up. And by the way, he says Scott's a creep."

"I believe that."

"You're still coming to the wedding?"

"How could I refuse?"

"Make a note of it."

◇

Not for the first time it occurred to me that I didn't know Just Watson. We were sitting in his study looking out over the west yard as the sunlight faded. He was somehow austere even in his weakened condition. Perhaps because of it he encouraged that perception now, I thought. For a brief moment I wondered how far he would go to protect his reputation. Then I put the thought out of my mind.

I had come by to see if I could get him anything for supper. He asked for rice and beans and some fried plantains from one of the Cuban restaurants. And a flan for dessert. I called and placed the order, then drove over and picked it up. I ate with him. Then we sat quietly, watching the dying light.

The house was silent. Ardis had removed her possessions. The judge was back living alone in his study. Did he want it that way, or had he truly felt forced, out of fear, to revert to the kind of life he understood? I didn't know and probably never would.

"Bud, have you seen Webb recently?" the judge suddenly asked.

I was taken by surprise. I don't know that we had ever talked about Webb.

"As a matter of fact I had lunch with him today."

"Webb's an old friend of yours, isn't he?"

"We were close at one time, but not so much now."

Just nodded and continued to stare out the window. After a while he said, "Too bad. You went separate ways, I suppose."

"Once Peggy and I were divorced, we lost touch. It wasn't a falling out, just ..." I left it unfinished. I didn't know what it was. Or it was a lot of things that I didn't want to dredge up now.

More silence. The light grew dimmer until Just finally reached over and turned on the lamp on the desk. "I hear he's having problems."

"I talked to Peggy the other day and she mentioned something to that effect."

"He doesn't talk about it?"

I shrugged. "Not really. Marital stuff, I think. We don't have that kind of a relationship anymore." Out of fairness to Webb, I didn't want to bring up his involvement with the escort service.

"It's too bad," Just said.

I thought he was talking about Webb's problems. "He'll work through it."

"I meant your friendship. It's a hard thing to come by and sad to see it dissolve."

"I guess we all change." I felt a certain awkwardness.

The silence wrapped around us with the encroaching darkness. Just seemed preoccupied while I pondered our conversation. At nine I got up to leave. "You need anything?"

Just looked up at me as if unaware anyone else was in the room. He shook his head.

"Call if you do; I'll check in with you in the morning."

"Thanks, Bud." He extended his hand. We shook. I gathered up the dishes, carried them out to the kitchen, and washed up before leaving.

Back home I was restless. Something about that conversation with the judge wouldn't leave me. I paced back and forth, sat at the piano and played a few bars before beginning to pace again.

At ten-thirty I sat down at the desk and looked up Webb's home phone number, a number that years ago I had known by heart. I picked up the phone, then put it down. Five minutes later I picked it up again. Judy answered on the third ring. She sounded as if she might have been asleep.

"Is anything wrong?" Judy's voice still sounded adolescent to me. The last time I saw her she had grown stout, but her face looked just as it had when we were in high school together, as if nothing had happened to her in nearly forty years.

"I don't think so. I just wanted to talk to Webb."

"He's working."

I was surprised. Webb had reached the point in his career with the sheriff's department where he no longer had to pull night duty. "He's not out on patrol, surely?"

"No, something private."

"Do you know when he'll be in?"

"He thought around midnight. Do you want me to have him call you?"

"No, I'll catch up with him. He tell you what the gig was?"

"Something at the Pier House I think he said. You're sure there isn't any trouble?"

"Positive. I'd just hoped to chat with him."

Peggy no doubt had mentioned to Judy that she had asked me to talk to Webb, but Judy wouldn't say anything. Too many years had gone by for that kind of intimacy between us. "It's nothing," I said. "I'll call him tomorrow."

"You're sure?"

"Of course."

She hesitated as if she wanted to say something but couldn't. Finally, we both just said good-night.

After hanging up, I got the keys to the Buick and went out the back way to a side street where the car was parked. I had no idea why I was doing this except that I wasn't tired and knew I wouldn't sleep if I went to bed. As far as I knew, the judge had been talking idly, making conversation, but it had awakened some instinct in me. I thought if Webb was just standing around, on guard duty for some private party, he might welcome my company.

Putting the Buick in a spot next to a black Lincoln Town Car in the parking lot, I got out to roam around the grounds in search of Webb. Probably I could have gone to the front desk of the Pier House and asked where he was, but I was in no particular hurry.

Two couples who had had too much to drink were in the pool splashing around and making a lot of noise when I went by. A security guard came over and pointed at his watch, but the drunks ignored him. The guard was trying to reason with them as I followed the walkway beyond the pool and back through a narrow tangle of foliage. In the distance I could hear canned music drifting up from one of the beach bars.

I paused, leaning against the smooth trunk of a coconut palm tree, staring across at a separate wing of the hotel, then realized I was looking at the building where I had come in search of Brendan Scott a few days ago. I was about to go on toward the beach when I saw the door open in that same building: Scott came out, followed by Webb Conners.

Twenty-five yards away and in the shadows, I was almost certain that I could not be seen by them. I watched the two men come down the steps of the building, Scott carrying a plastic glass, a cigarette wedged in the corner of his mouth. Webb was out of uniform, naturally, wearing a pair of slacks and a flowery tropical shirt that made him look even larger than usual.

The path I had followed split into a Y midway between where I was standing and the building Webb and Scott had just left. Easing back into the darkness of the shrubbery, I watched as the two men walked in my direction. If they passed by me, I thought it unlikely they would see me, but nevertheless, I felt some relief when they took the other leg of the Y, which wound around the beach area and eventually came out in the parking lot where I had left the Buick. I let a few seconds go by and followed.

Scott stopped at the open-air bar on the beach and had his glass refilled, while Webb, looking ill at ease, waited beside him. I hung back until they continued down the path, disappearing between two buildings in the direction of the parking lot. Hurrying, I came out on the edge of the lot in time to see them approach the Town Car next to my Buick.

They stood for a moment by the driver's door, talking. Webb took something from Scott, who then opened the door and got in. Webb waited for Scott to back out before walking across the parking lot in the opposite direction from where I stood.

I hustled over to the Buick, cranked up the engine, and backed out. I had seen Scott turn onto Duval Street, but right now I was more interested in Webb. The parking lot extended around the Pier House's office, which was the direction Webb had walked. On the chance that he had been going to his own vehicle, I wound through the lot slowly and got lucky. I spotted Webb's late-model pick-up—he had always driven a pickup—exiting the lot onto Front Street, heading down to the Simonton Street inter-section where Webb turned right, apparently in no par-ticular hurry.

I followed at a distance through the quiet streets across town to another upscale hotel, where Webb parked and got out. I watched from the curb as he walked inside, then left my car and sauntered across the grounds. The hotel was large, with a late-night bar that catered to tourists and hookers. From a window I could see Webb seated away from the bar at a table with a couple of plush chairs. In the other chair, opposite Webb, was a woman half his age in a red dress. She was running the toe of one high heel slowly up the back of his calf.

Webb looked around the bar nervously, but no one seemed to be paying any attention to him. I walked in, sat at the bar, and ordered a club soda. I positioned myself so that Webb would see me when he turned to look my way, as I was sure he would, but not so that there would be eye contact. I wanted to give him the opportunity to come to me on his own.

A couple of guys in suits, their ties askew, were at the other end of the bar, their sports talk occasionally drifting across to me. Midway along the bar two women dressed for an evening out sat smoking and talking, their gestures as languid as the smoke that curled from their cigarettes. They checked out the guys in the suits, then glanced in my direction but apparently saw no future in me.

Fifteen minutes later I was aware of some commotion in the corner where Webb was seated. I didn't look that way. A few minutes later the woman in red left the bar, looking none too happy. I ordered another club soda.

Five minutes dragged by, then ten. There was no way

out of the room without passing the bar. The guys in suits ordered fresh drinks and seemed to notice the languid ladies for the first time. Soon they were all sitting together, having a fine time.

When Webb came over, he put a hand on my back, smiling as if this were quite a coincidence. "Bud, what the hell you doing here?"

I stared at him, watching the smile disappear. "Why don't you sit down, Webb. I think we need to talk."

34

◇

It was like old times. Webb and I side by side at the bar. We had whiled away afternoons, and not a few long nights, swilling beer and shots of rum while Peggy and Judy waited up abstemiously for us, trying to laugh it off, until over the years it had gone on once too often and their humor turned to rancor.

Webb and I began our drinking careers together, in high school, starting with a filched beer or two from the fridge at the home of one of our parents, along with the occasional sweet burning hits from their rum bottle. Nothing more than boyish adventures, except that Webb and I both developed a taste for the stuff, enough so that by the time he was a junior, Webb, who was a big, fast, muscular kid and starting fullback, was dropped from the varsity football squad. Our grades suffered and we both barely managed to graduate, after which Webb pulled himself together sufficiently to get into a junior college for a year or so while I went to Korea.

When I returned, Webb had married Judy, and I picked
up with Peggy, my high school sweetheart. Webb was
working for the sheriff's department then, and we soon
reestablished our old habits, carrying on for a few years
until Webb was threatened with the loss of his job and his
marriage unless he quit drinking. He stopped, got into a
program, and basically settled down, while I continued
the wayward life.

Over the years, I watched as Webb ballooned up, his
appetite for food apparently as gargantuan as it had once
been for booze. Although the years had changed us and
we had followed separate paths, it was impossible not to
look back from time to time and recapture those moments
of pure youthful indulgence when we had an unwavering
friendship, an understanding of one another that was as
close and true a bond as I had ever had. We were truly
brothers, and I had never since had the experience of that
kind of male brotherhood. Neither, I was sure, had Webb.

I thought about that, sitting at the bar with this man
from whom I'd grown so distant.

Webb's hand trembled slightly as he raised the glass of
rum to his mouth.

"When did you start drinking again?"

"I don't know, Bud, maybe six months ago. Nothing
serious, just a drink now and again. It's not a problem."

I knew how wrong Webb was, but I also knew better
than to argue with him over that point. "Does Judy
know?"

Webb shook his head.

"What's going on with you?"

Webb stared down at his drink, his large, puffy hands
engulfing the glass.

"I wish to hell I knew, Bud. I really do."

"Women?"

Webb's shoulders hunched as if he would like to retract

his neck, turtlelike, and hide. "I can't seem to get out of it, Bud, it's worse than booze. Look at me sitting in here. What is it, midnight for Christ's sake?" Webb looked up, turning toward me. "You saw the babe, right?"

I nodded. Webb now had a twin addiction. At one time I might have been an influence. Now I could only listen.

"I thought I could walk away from it, especially when you confronted me after Katy died. I told myself that's it. It's got to stop. I believed it." Webb shook his head back and forth as if he were trying to get rid of something.

The bartender, looking like a bridegroom in his white shirt and black bow tie, his sleeves rolled up, came over and inspected my empty glass. I gave him the nod and watched him pick up the glass and fill it. When he put it in front of me, he looked at Webb before turning and walking away. At the other end of the bar, the ladies who had been so bored earlier were coming to life with their new friends in the suits.

"But what are you doing here, Bud, at this time of night?"

I sensed Webb's weight shift as his foot began to tap on the rung of the barstool, sending quivers of flesh dancing around his middle. He drained his glass, then held on to it, twisting it in his hands.

I took a drink of soda water. "You know a guy by the name of Brendan Scott?"

Webb's glass clattered against the bar. His flesh continued to jump in time to his foot's jiggle. He turned to me, his face scarlet. I saw something in his eyes that I'd never seen there before, more than simply fear: a look of doomed resignation. I felt sorry for my old friend, but I'd gotten into this and now I had to get to the bottom of it.

"You're not here by coincidence, are you, Bud?"

I shook my head. "I called Judy earlier this evening. She said you were working something private at the Pier

House. I thought you might have liked some company."

Webb looked as low as a basset hound with stomach acid. He stared at the bottom of his glass and grimaced. "Bud, I've got money problems."

"How bad is it?" I knew nothing of Webb's financial situation. He and Judy owned their home, a couple of vehicles. They had no children and, as far as I knew, lived on Webb's salary from the sheriff's department.

"I've gone through most of our savings in the last year."

"Does Judy know about it?"

Webb shook his head. "I've been moonlighting, trying to replace it before she finds out."

"I guess I don't have to ask where it all went."

Webb didn't say anything. He didn't have to. It went out the door with the gal in the red dress. Sex, like food and booze, had found its way onto Webb's list of addictions.

"And you were moonlighting for Scott?"

"I'd rather not talk about that, Bud."

"Help me here, Webb. This is between you and me. It doesn't have to go any further."

"Look, Bud, you're a private. You of all people should understand this kind of thing."

"What I understand, Webb, is that you've been compromised. Whatever Scott's using you for, he's got you by the short hairs. What you've got to understand is that I do, too. Think about it. Just how vulnerable you are right now. You couldn't afford to say no to him, and you can't afford to say no to me."

Webb hesitated, staring down at his empty glass. "God, Bud, we've been friends a long time. A lot of water under the bridge."

"Enough."

"You ever think back all those years and wonder what happened to us?"

I nodded. "Tell me about Scott. If you're in trouble, Webb, maybe I can help."

"One time maybe you could have. Not now."

"Try me."

The bartender moved toward us and Webb extended his glass. The bartender took the glass, then brought a bottle up from the shelf and free-poured. Webb stared down at the amber liquid. I pushed five dollars from my change across the bar and the bartender disappeared with it.

Webb sipped his drink, held it in front of him, then took a longer drink.

"Does it have to do with Katy?"

Webb nodded.

"What was Scott's connection to her?"

Webb looked away from his drink for a moment. "You don't know that?"

"No one ever bothered to tell me."

Webb's foot began to jiggle again. "Katy was his daughter."

I took a deep breath, trying not to show my surprise. For the second time that day I thought of Katy standing in my office, saying she had only recently come to know her father. "He told her?"

"I don't know who told her. From what I heard, she was pretty upset by it." The drink wasn't helping Webb's anxiety level.

I turned away to mull over this revelation, unsure how drunk Webb was and how much more I would be able to coax from him. Besides being drunk, he was nervous and scared. I knew him well enough to see that.

A certain anxiety of my own struck me. "Webb, what were you doing for Scott?"

Abruptly Webb stood up. "Let's get out of here."

We walked out of the bar, Webb lumbering, slightly unsteady, and across the hotel lobby and out the front door, crossing the circular driveway toward Webb's pickup where we were concealed by darkness. Webb put his foot up on the running board as if to steady himself.

"Scott's a pirate," Webb said. "He's protecting his investment."

"What did he need you for?"

"I've done work for him in the past, Bud. Checking out investors, that sort of thing. There's a lot of mistrust in that business. You can understand. He had called me recently about that chalice and asked me to help recover it."

"What did you have to do, Webb?"

"Keep tabs on people."

"What people?"

Webb stared at me. "You and Katy." He climbed in the truck and closed the door, then rolled down the window. "Watch your ass around Scott."

I watched him through the open window as he fumbled for the keys. Then I turned and walked toward my car. I heard him call to me when I was halfway between his vehicle and mine. When I turned, Webb's face was framed in the open window of his pickup as he leaned slightly forward, inserting the key in the ignition. His face carried a wistful expression, I thought, as if the years could somehow be made to disappear, and we would once again be innocent pranksters. Best buddies. "Sorry, Bud," he said.

I lifted my hand to wave good-bye, and as I did, I saw Webb's face contort into a grimace of pain and surprise, as if it had suddenly been jolted by an electrical shock and frozen in time.

35

◇

Rushing back to the pickup, I pulled Webb from behind the driver's seat and laid him on the concrete. A couple was entering the hotel and I shouted to them to call 911 and get an ambulance. Then I began pounding on Webb's heavy chest with the palm of my hand.

With the rhythmic, monotonous exercise I felt a tightening in my own chest as my breath became shallow and labored. I had a sense of suspension, as if I were swimming, fearful that if I stopped hammering on Webb's chest, my own heart would stop.

When the paramedics arrived, I was still pushing on Webb's heart, unaware that I was talking to him until I was pulled off by one of the medics. Another one bent over Webb, checking his eyes, his pulse, while I stood by and watched, rendered helpless now.

The other medic got the defibrillator from the back of the ambulance, brought it over, and attached the pads to

Webb's chest. Several volts of current bounced through his body, shaking him like so much Jell-O.

A small crowd had gathered, and when the police arrived, I felt as if I had suddenly regained consciousness. I was surprised to see Bill Eberhardt there. "Gideon, were you with Webb?"

I nodded.

"Jesus God, what happened?"

"We were talking in the bar and I walked him to his truck. I guess he had a heart attack." I didn't want to say much more, realizing now that I had to think of Judy, to try to protect her.

One of the medics came over. "Nothing we can do. It must have been massive. He went like that." The medic snapped his fingers.

Webb was dead. In a daze, I drove the Buick home, parked, and walked up the alley to the back entrance.

Tom came up on the back porch and whispered around my ankles as I opened the back door. I reached for the light switch, but before my hand closed on it I was blinded by the sudden light from a flashlight. A voice said, "Don't move!"

Blinking, I tried to look beyond the light, but I could see nothing except a dark figure holding the high-intensity flashlight at eye level. He lowered the beam for a moment so that I could see his other hand; a gun was pointed at my chest.

We stood there like ancient stone carvings in a dark tableau, and just as mute. The cat had followed me in and lay at my feet, motionless, staring up at the light. I knew I hadn't interrupted any ordinary burglary in progress. Whoever was on the other end of the flashlight had been waiting for me. I thought I knew why.

"You're going to walk in the bedroom and open that safe now." The voice was barely above a whisper.

Yep, I knew why all right. I wished I knew who. And maybe I did.

"I don't keep any money in the safe."

"I didn't ask you what you keep in there. I just said you're going to open it."

I started to move forward.

"Hold it! Put your hands and forehead on the refrigerator."

"I'm not hungry."

"Forget the wisecracks. I don't have a sense of humor."

I leaned my face against the refrigerator as the guy put the light on the table, its beam on me, then came over behind me and patted me down. When he was satisfied that I wasn't armed, he picked up the light and came back and jabbed the gun barrel into the small of my back. "All right, now just walk in there real slow and don't try to be a hero."

We went into the bedroom and I knelt down on the floor in front of the safe. It was an old combination safe, made of prewar steel. A safecracker could probably have gotten into it without difficulty, but this guy wasn't a safecracker. He would have been expecting to find what he was looking for out in the open; when he didn't, he must have reasoned that it was in the safe and it would be faster and easier to put a gun in my back and let me get at it rather than coming back later.

I fiddled with the knob in the glare of the light coming over my shoulder, deliberately missing the combination a couple of times as I stalled, trying to think. If Scott or Delgado was behind this, my life wouldn't be worth much when the burglar had gotten what he wanted.

"Come on, pal, let's get it open."

I spun the dial again. "Okay, okay. It's temperamental in its old age—like me."

"I don't need excuses. Just open it."

I clicked on the numbers, feeling the tumblers fall into place. I reached for the handle and turned it, and the heavy door opened silently. The flashlight beam stabbed the dark interior of the safe. My personal papers were stacked in there and the box with the wine chalice in it. I had to assume he knew what he was looking for.

"Take everything out and put it on top of the safe." I felt the gun jab a little farther into the soft flesh below my ribs. I did what he asked, putting the box with the pile of papers, all on top of the safe. "Now close the door." I pushed it closed.

The guy had the gun in one hand, the flashlight in the other, and some stuff to go through—plus me to deal with. Until he found the cup, I figured he still needed me. But I wondered how he was going to juggle it all. In the silence, he seemed to be wondering the same thing. Finally, he said, "Okay, pal, stretch out on the floor, facedown."

He kept the light on my face as I lay down on the dusty hardwood floor in the narrow room, lying between the bed and the piano. I got a noseful of dust and sneezed. I wiped my nose on my sleeve, lying with my head and arms at the opposite end of the room away from the safe.

"Rest easy for a minute, pal."

The light swung away from my face back to the top of the safe. With my cheek on the floor I could just see him out of the corner of one eye. He scattered the papers on the floor. His face was still in shadow, but I could just make out of the sharp profile. I recognized him, confirming what I'd already suspected. It was the punk who'd been following me around. He briefly flicked the light on me, then brought it back to the top of the safe.

Reaching my right hand down along my side, my fingers closed on one of the spindle legs of the piano stool. The guy had put the gun on top of the safe. I heard him grunt with some satisfaction as he picked up the box. My moment was at hand.

Lurching sideways, I launched the piano stool one-handed with as much force as I could muster. It struck him in the middle of his back, enough to knock him off-balance and give me a chance to get to my knees. Grabbing him around his legs, I pulled him back.

He stumbled against the piano, one hand slamming into the keys, causing a discordant ringing. I tried to hammer him in the nuts with my fist; he groaned but took a step back, grabbing a handful of my hair as I tried to struggle to my feet.

I was halfway up, trying to knee him, when something slammed against my head, and I drifted out on a fast current to nowhere.

36

◇

When I came to, I had a knot the size of a golf ball on the side of my head near my right ear and a feeling akin to seasickness in the pit of my stomach. I staggered up, assessed the damage and the time, determined there was nothing I could do until morning, and took some aspirin before going to bed. When I awoke the next time, sunlight was streaming in the bedroom window and the phone was ringing. I closed my eyes and coughed, tasting bile. The phone stopped ringing. I struggled up, my head feeling as if someone were inside it with a jackhammer. I looked at the clock and saw that it was after nine.

I took a shower and put water on for coffee, then sat at the kitchen table with an ice pack held against the lump on my head. Three cups of coffee, several more aspirin, and an hour later I was almost ready to face the day.

No messages were on the answering machine. I sat down at the desk and was reaching for the phone when it rang.

"Why the hell didn't you tell me that kid was Jack Whelan's son?" Joe Delgado's voice was breezy. Too breezy for the way I felt.

Through the throbbing in my head it took me a minute even to decipher what he was talking about. Then I remembered that today was Patrick's first day of work for Delgado.

"So what," I growled.

"You don't sound so good. Anything wrong?"

"Yeah, something's wrong. I've got a goose egg on the side of my head and a bad taste in my mouth."

Delgado laughed. "I've had a few mornings like that myself. Try a little hair of the dog."

"I don't drink. I think I've just been keeping bad company."

"Tell me, who you mad at, Gideon?"

"I think it wouldn't be too hard to work up some anger at you, Joe. This goose egg seems to have your name on it."

"Gideon, Gideon. I don't like to hear that. What happened?" His carefree tone nudged the pain in my head a little deeper. I could practically see that wine chalice sitting in front of him, glinting while Delgado smirked.

"What happened is the punk you—or Scott—hired to tail me broke into my place last night. He was waiting for me when I got back here."

"What punk? We've been through this. I told you I didn't hire anyone to tail you."

"You and Scott are like twins in my mind. I've ceased making any distinction."

"Wait a minute, Gideon. Let's back up here. Describe him, the guy who attacked you."

I described the kid whom I had cornered the other day; despite the darkness, I was sure he was the same person who had gotten in here last night.

"No. Definitely no. Not me and not Scott. Gideon, believe me, we didn't have anyone on you like that."

"How about Webb Conners?"

Delgado hesitated, slowing down as if the wind had suddenly been stripped from his sails. When he spoke, his voice had changed. "Webb Conners," he drawled. Another hesitation. And then: "You've talked to Webb?"

"Last night. Just before he died."

"Died?"

"I think he had a heart attack. I met him at a hotel after he'd reported to Scott. Webb wasn't well. He was drinking again. He had a lot on his mind. He was an old friend of mine. This wasn't a pretty end."

"Gideon, it was Scott's idea. He thought we needed some extra leverage, keeping up with the police investigation. And everything."

"Everything being me."

"I wish you wouldn't take it personally."

"I wish I didn't have this headache. I wish Webb was still alive. I don't hold you responsible for either one of those things, but there are other things you may be accountable for. I can't work for you any longer. I'll draw you up an invoice, but as far as I'm concerned, you don't owe me anything. It's quits. *Kaput.*"

"What about Katy?"

"What about her? It would have been helpful if I'd known who her father was, but you wouldn't even give me that."

"Gideon, I—"

"There's really nothing more to say. I think I'll go take some more aspirin. The headache's getting worse."

"Gideon, there's still that wine chalice."

"There was. It went out of here last night with the punk kid."

I had to pull the phone away from my ear. Delgado's

response was like the wail of some wounded animal trapped inside an echo chamber. "You had it! You didn't tell me!"

"I had it for twenty-four hours. I've been working on an investigation. I didn't have time to tell you."

"Where'd you get it?"

"I don't work for you anymore, remember? Now I've forgotten why you called. Something about Patrick Whelan."

Delgado swore. When he spoke, he sounded as pained as I was, as if someone had hit him in the head with a bat. In a manner of speaking, I suppose I had. "His old man practically revolutionized the salvage industry with his inventions."

"You don't say."

"Listen, Gideon, I'll have Bren get in touch with you."

"Yeah, do that. I'll look forward to it like a snake bite."

And hung up.

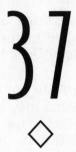

37

◇

I had to talk to Judy and Peggy, who both called within five minutes of each other.

"Oh, Bud, why!" were the first words Judy uttered when I answered. I didn't tell her he had been drinking, or why I'd gone looking for him. I could see no reason now why the secrets Webb had been burdened with shouldn't go with him to the grave. I made up some story about Webb and me stopping off at the hotel after he'd finished his stint. Maybe the coroner would be kind and keep the fact that Webb was drinking from his report, but either way I could do nothing about that.

When Peggy called, I had an almost instant replay, which I terminated before she could begin dragging details from me with her endless questions. Afterward, I called the judge and told him everything.

"It's good you saw him last night," Just said.

"I probably wouldn't have if it hadn't been for our conversation earlier."

Just didn't say anything. I asked him if he wanted me to come by, if he needed anything, and he said no, he was fine. I pictured him still sitting in his study, staring out the window. And wondered what he thought about while he sat there.

Then I tried reaching Ardis but only got through to an answering machine. I left a message that I'd be playing tonight at the club, the first of the Easter gigs was beginning, and reminded her that she had once expressed an interest in hearing me play.

The headache left me restless, and only by reclining did the pain ease somewhat. I lay on the couch in the office thinking about Webb and the judge. And Brendan Scott, who, according to Webb, was Katy's father.

Katy knew that Scott was her father when she went out with me. She'd been bothered by that knowledge, but something else had triggered her ultimate depression. The anger and despair I'd witnessed in her Saturday night in the club. Something she'd learned from Delgado had left her totally despondent. What was it? And what about the chalice? I wondered. Was it because of Scott's being her father that she felt she had a claim to it? And where did Webb Connors fit into all of this?

Webb had been a perennial presence in the courthouse. He had spent most of his adult life wandering its halls, bantering with the clerks' and judges' secretaries, wheedling and gossiping. Webb knew not only the nooks and crannies of the buildings that house Monroe County's seat of information but also many of the secrets of our citizens. In short, he had access.

I had never thought of Webb and the judge as being friends, but given the timing of Just's conversation last night, and Webb's subsequent confession, I began to wonder just how friendly they might have been.

There was Webb: best friend, old buddy. A guy who'd

do anything for you. Stolid, mild-mannered Webb, who, somehow, somewhere along the line, had lost control, had gotten in over his head, and felt forced, for financial reasons, to take on questionable outside work.

I wondered how much the judge knew about Webb's moonlighting.

Then there was Delgado. His response, when I told him about the theft of the wine chalice, lent substance to his denial of knowing about the punk who stole it. Of course I had to consider the possibility that Brendan Scott was behind that theft, operating independently of Delgado.

And what about Delgado's information about Ardis's husband, Jack? I lay there trying to sift and sort and not think about my head injury, and how it got there. I drifted. Finally, sometime around noon I pulled myself away from pity and pain and decided to get out of the house.

I put on an old soft cap, mostly to conceal the lump on my head, and biked down to the waterfront with a vague idea of looking in on Patrick. It was as still and hot as it had been yesterday, and by the time I got down there I had worked up a sweat, which seemed to help clear my senses. No one was around the boat, but I could hear tinny music coming from inside before I decided I didn't want to see Patrick after all.

Matt Johnson was asleep on a bench in the shade on the lee side of the fuel docks, a half-empty wine bottle for a pillow, one arm dangling lifelessly off to the side. White stubble dotted his face, his lips shivered intermittently when he breathed, and a thread of drool ran down his chin. He was drunk, sleeping it off, and I rode on past without waking him.

Riding up the street, I saw Fred Pacey from two blocks away heading back to his office. Slowing down I timed it so that we would intersect just when he got to his building.

"Fred, what a coincidence," I said, stopping my bike so that it blocked the entrance to the building.

Pacey looked annoyed. Colorful suspenders held up his well-pressed slacks. He didn't have on a jacket and his fine white pima-cotton shirt looked as if he had just put it on. His tasseled loafers gleamed. A halo of sunlight crowned his bare head.

"Webb Conners died last night. Did you hear?"

Pacey looked over my shoulder and sort of shook his head no.

"Apparently Webb was moonlighting for a guy named Brendan Scott, who's got an interest in a major salvage operation."

Pacey didn't react; if he was rattled by that information, he didn't show it. On the other hand he wasn't exactly the sort of guy who showed anything. I had seen him get angry the last time we talked, but I knew that was just for appearance' sake, the sort of thing corporate guys do whenever they're feeling threatened.

"I understand you were an investor in Scott's operation."

"Where'd you hear that?" Pacey checked his fingernails.

"It appears Webb had been keeping good track of Scott's investors. Making sure they were in for the long haul is how I read it."

"I get the feeling you're trying to tell me something, Gideon. Why not save us both some time and lay it out. I'm a busy man."

"Of course Webb wasn't above working both sides of the street. He was desperate. He might have come to a man like you, figuring perhaps you could use someone like him. Just to let you know that he was available in the event that you needed him."

A rapid, almost imperceptible tic wrinkled the corner

of Pacey's left eye and then was gone. But it was enough to bolster my courage.

"You acknowledged the other day that Katy Morgan had something she wanted to sell you."

Without responding, Pacey forced a tight smile to cross his mouth.

"It's possible to believe you might have known more about that object than you let on the other day." Pacey was an investor. He might have known about the chalice. Or else he was stringing her along to avoid embarrassment to his family.

"I've got to go. I've got appointments." He made a move toward the entrance. I leaned the bike inward. Pacey gave me a look that would have turned water to ice in August.

"Sorry if I stepped on your toes. But if I were you, I'd stay on them." Saluting, I rode off.

38

◇

Jack Whelan? Yeah, I knew him. Guy thought he knew everything. Problem was he didn't know when to shut up." Captain Easy talked while he was bent over one of the ship models, squinting through a pair of half-glasses as he threaded a piece of line through a yardarm.

He seemed glad to see me, ready to talk to anyone who had an interest in diving, the salvage industry, or related matters. I was interested in related matters. Like Jack Whelan.

"He was one smart bastard. I'll give him that." Captain Easy was a study in controlled motion. He was like a watchmaker and a puppeteer rolled into one. I could see every flexed muscle in his powerful forearms, the controlled finger movements, and the exquisite concentration in the set of his face—everything articulated, perfectly coordinated, all as he talked as if he were doing nothing more than changing a lightbulb.

"I heard he revolutionized the salvage industry," I said.

Easy fitted a small clamp to the yardarm, his tongue protruding. When he finished, he said, "Yeah, maybe some exaggeration, but he definitely left his mark. Like the underwater metal detectors and the device for using the propeller wash for moving sand. Jack had a big part in that."

"He didn't live here though."

"Nope. Came a month or two every winter but always with some new idea to try out."

"You like him?"

"Like him? What the hell. I didn't know him. I got a job to do. He does his thing. We never sat around shooting bullshit."

"What happened to him?"

"What happened?" Easy looked at me quizzically. "Hell, he died. Like what happens to all of us."

"I mean with the inventions. He make any money?"

"Hell, no. I told you. He talk too much. The company gets a patent on the stuff. Jack gets points in the company. Then he died. Next thing you know the company make the big score. Jack shoulda kept some stuff to himself. Then he had something to sell. You know what I mean?"

"Yeah, I know what you mean. Was he angry?"

"Angry." Easy snorted. "Mad like a bee. He get a lawyer and take them to court, but he got nothing, no foot to stand on because all he did was talk. Got nothing on paper. No agreement. Stupid, no?"

I agreed that it wasn't too bright, then sat in silence for a while watching Captain Easy work. It felt good sitting in here under the bare bulb hanging from the rafters, surrounded by wood shavings, the smell of glue and resin, watching the gradual re-creation of something that no longer existed, even if it was in miniature. Listening to Easy talk in his slightly fractured English was somehow comforting.

For a time, while he worked, we talked about other things until I said I had to leave. Easy told me to come back anytime. "You're good company, Bud, even though you got much on your mind."

I went home and called Tim Kelly. His secretary answered and in the background I could hear the jackhammers tearing up the street and more faintly the overlay of music from her CD. She recognized me. "Oh, yes, hold on. I'll see if he's available."

I held for five minutes, then Kelly's voice said, "Gideon, how goes the detecting business?"

"By any chance did you represent Jack Whelan?"

There was a silence. I sensed I'd taken him off guard. "Why, yes, I did."

"I'd like to know more about that."

Kelly coughed. "Sorry, Gideon, I'm not at liberty."

"Why not? Whelan's dead."

"That may be, but it's an ongoing case and I'm not prepared to talk about it at this time."

"His wife?"

"Sorry, Gideon."

We hung up. I sat at the desk staring at the closed blinds covering the windows. Then I ate a couple of hardboiled eggs, swallowed two aspirin before going back out into the hot spring afternoon.

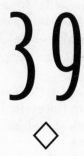

39

◇

Delgado didn't appear to be anywhere around the *Mariposa* when I arrived at the dock. And I could still hear the distantly familiar tinny music coming from the bowels of the salvage ship. I went aboard. The door to the companionway was open so I went below, following the sound of the music.

At the foot of the steps was a large table. Various charts were laid out on it, on many of which someone had drawn lines with meaningless numbers written beside them. Forward was a galley and a cold coffeepot on a gimballed stove. Various pieces of diving equipment were stashed here and there along with coiled ropes and marine stuff.

The ship seemed old, with rust spots bleeding through in some areas even though heavy layers of paint appeared to have been applied everywhere. Along the sides were panels with sliding doors and standing lockers. I opened a few of the doors and looked inside, finding nothing more interesting than store supplies and marine clothing.

I peeked into a cabin with four unmade bunks, and forward of that, a smaller enclosed cabin containing a head with a small stainless-steel sink, a toilet, and a shower, from which came the pungent smell of disinfectant.

Beyond was a bulkhead with a locked door. I retraced my steps, coming back to the stairs leading up to the deck and another companionway, which led aft. I followed the companionway, walking to the back of the ship toward the sound of the radio. Halfway back a ladder was built along one side of the engine room. It seemed to be unoccupied so I climbed down.

Two large twin diesels were mounted on doubled-up four-by-fours bolted to the ship's hull with a walkway that allowed access to both engines. The close air was nauseating. Farther astern was another bulkhead. I was standing listening to the music coming from back there when the door in the middle of the bulkhead opened and Patrick stepped into the engine compartment. He saw me and stopped, startled.

We hadn't seen each other since the night of the party at Just's, the night of the accident when I had taken Patrick on a midnight ride up the Keys and given him a history lesson. I wasn't sure how he would react to me. He looked different. For one thing his clothes were grimy, stained with paint. But mostly it was his face, his expression. Gone was that petulant look he had been wearing when we first met.

"What are you doing down here?" It wasn't asked in a challenging way.

"Taking a look at your job site. Thought I'd check up and see how you were doing."

Although he smiled, Patrick still had some adolescent awkwardness, and like his mother, he radiated nervous tension. I remembered how coaxing words from him was like trying to pry open a bank vault with a toothpick, but maybe the boy had something to say.

"Slinging paint isn't much fun, is it? You having second thoughts about what you want to do?"

"It's okay, and Mr. Delgado said he would teach me to dive. Tomorrow we're going out to a wreck site for a week."

"You think you can make a living as a diver?"

Patrick shrugged. "I can learn. I've got to get this job finished today though." He picked up a fresh can of paint that had been sitting outside the door.

"Mind if I come back there with you and see what you're doing?"

"The paint's wet, so be careful."

I followed him as he slouched through the bulkhead and into the aftermost part of the ship, where he was applying red paint to the interior of the steel hull. The closed space reeked of paint fumes and diesel fuel. Patrick turned off the blaring radio.

"I didn't know your dad had been involved in this business."

Patrick had his back to me as he began painting, but I could see his body tense up when I mentioned his father. "I don't really remember it." Patrick would probably have been only a baby when his father was experimenting with inventions.

"You know there was some controversy over his work, don't you? He felt he got screwed by one of the treasure outfits."

"I don't know much about it."

"Your mother never mentioned anything?"

"Not a lot." Certainly, Patrick hadn't inherited his father's talkativeness.

"You seen her recently, your mother?"

"Last night."

"She say anything about the judge?"

"She just said they weren't getting married right away."

"How do you feel about that?"

Patrick shrugged his shoulders as he continued to slap the thick paint on the hull. I knew that he would be embarrassed by the question, that he wouldn't have an answer, but for some reason I wanted to trip him up, wheedle something unexpected out of him.

I didn't say anything for a while, just stood in the companionway and watched him work. He didn't seem to be particularly uncomfortable to have me there. After a while I asked him if he had liked his father.

"He was okay."

"Just okay?"

He continued to paint but he seemed fidgety.

"Were you close?" I prodded.

"Not really."

"How would you describe him, your father?"

Patrick sighed. "Not there."

Good, I thought. You're on your way.

"Can we join the party?"

Somehow Delgado had managed to come up behind us without any announcement.

"I just stopped by to see the work conditions of my friend here. I'd say he needs a little more ventilation."

"Well, sure, I'll go right out and get an air conditioner. In the meantime I brought someone who'd like to have a word with you."

I looked over Delgado's shoulder. Brendan Scott was peering down the hatchway from the engine room.

40

◇

Sweat poured off Brendan Scott's brow, making rivulets down his jowly face. We sat at the chart table in the main cabin. Delgado had turned on a floor fan that shifted warm, moist air around our legs.

"We don't need to waste time on preliminaries," Scott said. "Joe, you got a Coke?"

Delgado went over to a refrigerator and brought a can of Classic back, popping the top and handing it to Scott. "Maybe Jughead here wants something."

I shook my head no.

Scott took a long drink from the can. "All right, then. I've been informed that you recently had something in your possession that we hired you to find."

I shook my head again.

"What's the matter?"

"There's been a misunderstanding. Joe here hired me to find out why Katy Morgan committed suicide." Delgado stood next to the table, scratching his head. "The treasure was incidental to the process. If and when that turned up, we were to negotiate a new contract. Isn't that right, Joe?"

"Something like that," Delgado said softly.

"But you didn't bother to inform us, did you?" Scott asked.

"I've been busy. I only had it for twenty-four hours."

"And then what happened?"

"I explained it all to Delgado. I thought one of your punks broke into my place and blindsided me."

Scott stared with bloodshot eyes across the table at me. "You expect me to fall for that?"

"I expect next to nothing from the two of you. And so far I haven't been disappointed."

"I took a dislike to you when you first forced your way into my room at the Pier House." Scott lowered his voice. "With time you haven't done anything to change that."

"So what are we going to do? Sit here and trade insults? You hired me to do a job. I did it until I found out I was being stonewalled. And spied on. Then I quit. That's where things stand right now."

Scott took another swig of Coke, then shook a Camel filter tip partially out of the pack, lifted the pack to his mouth, drew the cigarette out with his lips, and lit it with a Zippo lighter that produced a flame like a blowtorch.

Tossing his head back and exhaling smoke from his nostrils, he said, "We're not going to trade insults." He studied me through bulging, bloodshot eyes. "What we're going to do is have a little truth session. When we're done, if I'm not satisfied, you may find yourself providing some more ballast inside this tub."

I looked up at Delgado, but he wasn't smiling. "Fuck you," I said. "If we're going to play truth or consequences, I've got some questions of my own. Like why didn't I know about your relationship with Katy from the beginning?"

There was silence while Scott smoked. He devoured the cigarette as if he had been deprived of one for several days. Holding it close to his mouth, he no sooner expelled a lungful of smoke than he took in another. Smoking and breathing were all one. When he had smoked the cigarette down to the filter, he ground it out and turned to Delgado. "You got any rum? This Coke tastes flat."

Delgado opened a cupboard and carried a bottle of Appleton over to the table. Scott took another hit of Coke, then poured rum into the can, swirled it around, then took another hit and smacked his lips.

Scott looked at me. "You know who I am?"

"A three-time loser in matrimony with a hard-on for strippers and bar girls. A guy who likes racing fast boats while getting someone else to pay the bill for them. How am I doing so far?"

Scott laughed, looking at Delgado. "I told you this guy could turn in results. You missed a few stops along the way, but that's your problem. We're not here to talk about me."

Scott took another long drink.

"I'm here to talk about Katy Morgan," I said. "When was it she found out you were her father?"

"What difference does it make?"

"Plenty. People don't kill themselves for no reason. I'm trying to find Katy's reason. I think Katy took that chalice because she thought you owed her something. I've got another idea about why she took her life and it isn't very pretty."

Scott shot a glance toward Delgado. Then he laughed.

I didn't say anything. There wasn't anything to say.

"I thought we could work things out," Scott said. "Then the next thing I know she's dead and you're crawling around. She had that chalice and then you had it. All this other stuff is just bullshit. Now I'm giving you twenty-four hours to turn it up. If you don't, you're in a new line of business. One that won't require use of your legs."

"I finished painting, Mr. Delgado. Can I go now?" Patrick had come in and was standing in the companionway. I wondered how much he had heard.

"Sure, go home," Joe said. "Be back here, ready to leave the dock, at seven in the morning."

"Hang on, Patrick. I was just leaving myself." I stood up and walked over to the companionway.

"Twenty-four hours," Scott said. And lit another cigarette.

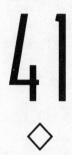

41

◇

The fresh air felt good after the smell of paint, oil, and diesel fumes mixed with sweat and Brendan Scott's Camels. I'd never felt comfortable on boats, even when they were tied to a dock.

"Got a little stuffy down there." I said to Patrick.

He nodded without saying anything. He seemed embarrassed, shy. He had an employer now, loyalties, and he'd just heard me threatened by that employer. He must have been uncomfortable.

"Where you headed?" I asked him.

"Another job."

That took me by surprise. After eight hours slinging paint inside the *Mariposa* it was the last thing I would have expected from Patrick. "Doing what?"

"Line handler for the cruise ship. One's leaving the dock today in just a few minutes."

Not a bad job. I'd watched the ships dock before; the crew members on board tossing thin lines to the line handlers on shore, who used those lines to retrieve the big hawsers that had to be fastened to the bollards, securing the ship. It usually took at least half an hour to get a ship tied up.

"How'd you get on there?"

Patrick shrugged. "The judge, I think. I've got to get over there now." He took off, running at a clip.

Amused at Patrick's newfound industriousness, I got on my bike and rode over to the adjacent dock where the sunset watchers had gathered. As I rode up, a mournful bellow erupted from the cruise ship, along with a puff of dark smoke from its stack.

A tugboat was standing by in the harbor to assist the ship. Passengers stood on the decks waving farewell while a small brass band played a calypso number, the notes getting lost in the noise of the ship and the crowd.

Patrick was working the stern lines with a couple of other guys while three other line handlers dealt with the bow lines. I watched for a while and was about ready to leave when a familiar face caught my attention.

I circled around the crowd, easing closer to the bow of the ship. One of the guys casting off lines was a tall, skinny kid in jeans and a navy blue T-shirt with a skull and crossbones printed on it. He and the two other boys grappled with the hawser, getting some slack and finally lifting it over the bollard while another kid tossed the thin retrieving line to the crew on the bow of the ship.

The kid in the blue T-shirt watched as the hawsers were gathered aboard and the ship crabbed away from the dock. Fifteen minutes later the ship was in the harbor, towering skyward like a floating hotel.

The kid had his hands on his hips, his profile to me. There was no doubt he was the punk who had tailed me all over town the other day, and, I would have bet my bicycle, the one who had left the knot on my head last night.

I worked my way back around the crowd and over to where Patrick was. He seemed surprised to see me.

"Thought I'd stick around and watch this. What do you get paid?"

"Twenty-five bucks."

I whistled. "Not bad for a half hour's work. Who pays you?"

"The shipping agency. They pay cash after every docking."

"By the way, do you know the kid in the skull-and-crossbones T-shirt working the bow lines."

Patrick glanced over there. "Not really. I think his name's Swann. That's all I've ever heard him called."

Swann. Something clicked. Like a pinball bouncing between cushions, finally circling the hole several times before slopping in with a clatter of bells.

"Thanks," I said. "You did a great job."

The ship bleated again, churning white water around the stern as the screws were reversed and the tug came over to push the bow around. The band continued to play as the crowd surged forward along the pier, getting ready for the sinking of the sun.

At home I went to my desk and found the papers I had gotten from Ms. Albury, Just's secretary. The upcoming court cases and the list of old cases going back ten years. Running my finger down each list, I found him. On both lists. Swann, Bill.

After a shower I cooked dinner and then got ready for an evening's entertainment.

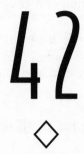

◇

At eight o'clock the club was quiet. Ronnie was standing behind the bar, looking beautiful and bored. Half a dozen people who were apparently stretching cocktails into the dinner hour laughed merrily in one corner. A couple of guys drinking shots and beer sat at one end of the bar; alone at the other end Pepper hovered over a cup of coffee. I sat down next to him.

"Gideon, right on time. I understand the town's full."

"Standing room only at sunset."

Pepper laughed. "Get them fed and they'll be ready for more liquor and some live entertainment."

Ronnie put club soda down in front of me. "Hi, Gideon." She smiled, then began worrying a fingernail between her teeth.

I carried the drink over to the piano, sat down, and fingered a few chords softly, then slid into a repertoire of soft melodic renditions of Sinatra hits, staying out of the way of the lingering group in the corner and the heavy drinkers at the bar, neither of whom were ready to be overpowered.

At nine, I took a ten-minute break, went to the men's room, and came back as the elevator doors opened and a dozen or so people swarmed into the room. Back at the piano I lifted the tempo, and within half an hour the place was smoke filled, laughter everywhere, the music filtering through it all providing a rhythm, some momentum to the night. By ten, as Pepper had predicted, the joint was jumpin'.

I didn't see Ardis come in, but when I took my next break, she was sitting at the bar. In the press of people I'm not sure I would have recognized her if she hadn't spoken to me.

"You're good, better than I expected." Ardis was sort of slumped at the bar, her normally perfectly coiffed hair was a mess, and she had on a rumpled pair of slacks and a blouse, not her usual immaculate attire. I realized she was on her way to being drunk.

Ronnie brought me a fresh club soda. I took her aside. "What's she drinking?" I motioned in Ardis's direction.

Beyond the glass windows the lights of the city twinkled. Dizzy Gillespie was blowing something lively from the CD.

"What's she drinking?" I repeated.

"Martinis, straight up." Ronnie winked."Bombay gin, Two olives."

I went back over to Ardis. She didn't look up. She was halfway through her drink, holding the martini glass by its stem in one hand, her little finger raised outward from the glass, delicate and ladylike, signifying some last vestige of respectability. Two olives rested at the bottom of the clear liquid, their pimiento red centers staring back at her like two crazed eyes.

"Ardis."

"I came to hear you play. Why aren't you playing?"

"In a moment. I'm on a break."

"Do you take requests?"

"If I know it, of course."

"Then I'd like to hear 'Love for Sale.' "

I studied her. "Is everything all right?"

Ardis's slightly glazed eyes stared into mine for what seemed like the first time since we had met. "Everything's just fine, just fine." The finality of her tone told me otherwise.

I started back to the piano, then stopped. "Ardis, I've got something I'd like to talk to you about."

She shook her head, as if clearing her mind of some tangled thought. She rested one hand on my forearm. "I thought you might." Her dry lips parted in what could have been either a smile or a grimace. "When do you want to talk? Tonight?"

"I won't get off until one o'clock."

Ardis took a drink. "Do you remember the night you came to dinner?"

I nodded.

"It seems like such a long time ago." She began to shake her head to some interior melody, her fingers drumming lightly against the bar. " 'A kiss is still a kiss.' Do you know that one, Gideon?"

" 'As Time Goes By.' Sure."

"Add that to the request list. If I'm going to stay here until you finish, I might as well listen to the songs I like."

I went back to the piano and began picking out the melody of the tune with my right hand, then added the left and brought them together. Ardis seemed to sit up straighter at the bar, her back to me. I saw her say something to Ronnie. A few minutes later Ronnie came over and put five dollars in my tip jar. I smiled. "See if you can get some coffee into her."

Ronnie lifted her hands and turned back to the bar as I segued into "Love for Sale." Oh, just so slightly soiled love for sale.

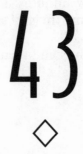

43

◇

The coffee was lukewarm in the cup. Ardis hadn't touched hers, but she hadn't had any more gin either. I took a hit of coffee. Ardis was sitting erect on her barstool, holding herself together somehow, as if she had to concentrate on every movement she made. She was balanced like an aerialist on the high wire; except that she was drunk. A tight little smile stayed on her lips, but her eyes were still glazed over.

It was one-thirty in the morning. People were still drinking, milling around, but most of the crowd had siphoned off gradually when I stopped playing, almost half an hour ago. "Try to get some coffee down, Ardis."

Ardis looked at me. She had had at least three martinis, Ronnie told me. "You think I'm drunk, Gideon?"

"What say we take a walk down to your car and I'll drive you home?"

"You don't think I can do it. Well, I'll show you." She stood up, wobbled, and put her hands on the barstool for

234

support. "Oh, I'm a mess." She bowed her head and dabbed at her eyes with the damp napkin.

"Come on. I'll help you." I put my arm around her waist and together we headed for the elevator.

Pepper was standing at the elevator, holding the door open. "You want me to go down with you?"

I shook my head.

In the elevator Ardis leaned against me, her hand on my chest, and when we came out on the ground floor and walked across the lobby, we must have looked like lovers after a long night on the town.

With some difficulty we found her car and I helped her into the passenger seat, then got behind the wheel of the little red sports car and drove her home. The house was dark. I assumed Patrick had already gone to bed, hoped that he had. I walked Ardis to the kitchen, asked her if she would like some more coffee.

"Will you have some, Gideon?"

"Sure."

"Because you want to get me sober so you can talk to me. It's always the same old story." Ardis tried to sing.

I put the coffeepot on.

"What do you want to talk about?" Ardis was seated at the kitchen table where Patrick and I had had our little talk the other night.

"I'd like to talk about Jack Whelan."

A brief glimmer of recognition appeared in Ardis's eyes. "Oh, yes, Jack. What do you want to know?"

I poured two cups of coffee and sat down facing her. It was going to be a long night, I thought. "I didn't know your husband was an inventor, that he'd played a part in the treasure-salvage industry here."

As Ardis tried to lift the cup to her mouth, a little coffee spilled onto the table. She put the cup back down without drinking. "That was a long time ago. I guess there's no reason you would have known."

"Not so long ago that there isn't a lawsuit still pending."

Ardis's eyes blinked several times, her head crooked to one side. "Where did you hear that?"

"People in the salvage business." I decided to wait before telling her that I had spoken to Tim Kelly.

Ardis lifted the cup and bent forward without spilling the coffee this time. "I can't drink any more of this. Excuse me, Gideon. I've got to go to the bathroom."

She stood up and walked out of the room, still a little unsteady, but without need of assistance. Five minutes later she came back. She had primped up a little. "Gideon, am I under suspicion of something?"

"No. I'm just trying to clear up some loose ends in another investigation."

Ardis carried her coffee cup over and dumped it in the sink. She came back and sat down and began laughing uncontrollably. Soon her head was down on the table and she was sobbing. I found a box of tissue and gave it to her. She sat up, dabbing at her eyes. "I'm sorry, I don't usually get like this."

"It wasn't such a happy little family as you portrayed, was it?"

"Gideon, why—"

"I spoke to Patrick earlier. I don't think he much cared for his father either."

Ardis bowed her head. "Jack wasn't an easy man."

"Was he broke when he died, Ardis?"

Ardis lifted a clenched fist to her mouth without answering me.

"When did the judge find out you weren't as financially stable as you'd led him to believe?"

"I don't know what you're talking about."

"Don't you? Why else would you be keeping that lawsuit alive?"

"It was important to Jack."

"Because he believed he was screwed out of some money?"

Ardis lowered her head, giving a little nod.

"So it's the principle of the thing then, not the money?"

"No. I mean—"

"This was once a small town, Ardis. Close-knit. People have always been friendly, but a little suspicious of strangers. I have to admit that when the judge first told me he was getting married to an outsider, my first thought wasn't charitable."

Ardis lifted her head, a trace of a smile on her face, but it wasn't happy. "I know that."

"I changed my mind about you after we met, but a lot of people are still wondering."

"I can't worry about what people think."

"Maybe you do worry about it."

She looked at me sharply. "What do you mean?"

"I think you want approval. Maybe the judge was a way of getting it."

"Please, Gideon!"

"After his accident, the judge changed. I thought he was simply trying to spare you the indignity of looking after an old man, but when he withdrew, I got suspicious. He wouldn't want to embarrass you, so he cut himself off, retreated, which was the one way he knew to deal with misfortune."

Ardis shifted in her seat.

"Don't worry, your secret's safe with me. You wanted some financial support and thought the judge could provide it, which he no doubt would have. Did you intend to stay with him?"

Ardis lowered her head. "I love him, Gideon. Why won't you believe me?"

"I want to. I really do. The judge deserves that much anyway."

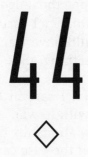

A rdis seemed to fold in on herself; we sat in silence, the only sound that of a slow drip from the faucet. I was beat. The lump on the side of my head still hurt and I felt as if I'd been on a weeklong binge.

Something was missing in Ardis's posture that I couldn't put my finger on. She wasn't sad, the way people who've had too much to drink can be, and I didn't feel the least bit sorry for her, but it occurred to me that the woman I'd first met over dinner at Just's was not the same woman who sat here now. I wondered which one was the real Ardis Whelan. She had been forceful enough, determined, if somewhat nervous around me back when we first met, but now she seemed lost—doomed was probably more like it.

All those years with a ne'er-do-well husband, trying to make the best of it while raising her son. Once Jack was dead, Ardis must have felt a certain freedom, even if she had loved him, but she was left with a son and little money. Then, along came the judge, combining integrity, respectability, and financial security. Everything a woman like Ardis would have wanted.

And there was something else. "Did you talk to Just about Jack's case?"

Ardis smiled bleakly. I saw in her expression something, some hesitant withdrawal. "I don't understand."

"Because of your relationship the judge would have had to recuse himself if the case came to him. You know that, don't you?"

"Gideon, how could you think—"

"But I suppose you might have hoped that he would put in a word for you with whoever was going to be the presiding judge."

Ardis closed her eyes. "You think I was just using him, don't you, Gideon?"

"Were you?"

She didn't open her eyes. She seemed to shiver as if she were cold, or recoiling from some terrible thought. "No, I loved him. Still love him."

She kept repeating her lines like a mantra. I could have made a cynical response to that, but I let it go.

The day the judge had come out of the hospital, I'd gone over to see him. I remembered coming out of his study with the clear impression that Ardis had been eavesdropping on our conversation. I tried to remember what it was Just and I had talked about. Whatever it was, it had been sufficient to change Ardis's mind about staying with him. It was the first time I had seen her show anything but stalwart support for him.

"Why did you leave then? The day he came out of the hospital."

"He didn't want me there. I wasn't going to cling to him. I have some pride left."

My coffee tasted bitter. I decided to try a different tack with Ardis. "Are you protecting him?"

Ardis offered another bleak smile. "Protecting Just? What do you mean?"

"After the car accident, something changed between the two of you. At first I thought it was because of the accident, but when it turned out that Just wasn't hurt badly, it didn't make any sense. Just tried to explain it by the age difference. You knew that he was eccentric, what his life had been like before you arrived, you had even explained his cold feet in going through with the marriage to me. So if you understood all of that, why did you leave so quickly? Unless you were protecting him. Or yourself."

"I told you, Gideon. I won't stay where I'm not wanted."

I shook my head. "You overheard my conversation with the judge the day he came from the hospital, didn't you?"

Ardis looked into the darkened next room as if someone were waiting for her. When she turned back, anger flashed in her eyes. "What if I did? He made it plain he wasn't going through with the marriage plans."

"But there was more than that. You heard all about my investigation into the death of Katy Morgan. I told the judge everything. And you already knew about his connection with Katy's mother because by then he'd told you."

"Yes, Gideon, he had. I got tired of always being locked out of your conversations. I demanded he tell me what was going on and he did. It was something in the past. I didn't judge him for it."

I nodded. "How did he explain Katy's death?"

"He didn't have an explanation. And I was careful not to demand any details. I know he was very disturbed about the effect this might have on Patrick."

"Did you ever hear the judge mention anyone by the name of Swann?"

Ardis seemed to roll the name around in her mind. "No, who is he?"

"A kid who works along with Patrick at the pier where the cruise ships dock."

"I know Just was helpful in getting Patrick that job. Is there some problem?"

There were a lot of problems, but I didn't want to spell them out to Ardis. She seemed tired now, but sober. It was almost three o'clock in the morning and I realized I had to walk home or call a cab. I decided to walk. Maybe the air would clear my head.

"You're so mysterious," Ardis said when I stood up. "I don't know whether to feel like a suspect or a poor witness."

"Neither. At least for the moment."

On the way home I walked by the judge's. The lights were out. I went on. My business with him could wait till morning.

45

◇

Thunder awakened me early the next morning. A steady, low rumble that shook the house and lasted for a minute or more before ending in a sudden, sharp explosion. The sky was battleship gray but there was no rain. I showered and dressed, grabbing a raincoat on my way out. I walked to the drugstore for a quick breakfast, then walked to the club to retrieve my bike.

The weather suited my mood. I was on my way to a reluctant confrontation, one that I would as soon have put off, even walked away from altogether. The judge was the closest thing to family I had left in Key West. A man can only take so much disillusionment before he learns to evade it, to sidestep it before tumbling over a precipice. I had been there before and taken the fall and I wasn't ready to do it again.

It was eight o'clock in the morning when I rode into the judge's side yard, leaning my bike against the inside of the brick wall that surrounded his house.

The rain was just beginning—big, slow-falling droplets that splattered like crushed fruit on the flagstone walkway as I made my way to the house. I glanced quickly into the window of Just's study where I could see him seated at his desk, a lamp on. I hurried toward the back entrance just as a flash of lightning rent the sky, followed by another seizure of thunder. I stepped inside the kitchen, leaving my poncho on a hook by the door, and walked down the hallway as the rain began to tumble down.

I knocked on the study door.

"Come in, Bud."

I pushed open the door. The judge turned slowly toward me. He was in his bathrobe. "I saw you coming across the yard." His expression was fixed, but something in his eyes and his uncombed hair made him look as if lightning had struck a little too close. "I was just writing my resignation letter."

"Why now?" I sat down in the overstuffed chair, its leather darkened with age.

Just turned to face me. "I thought I might go back for six months or so, but I've decided against it. I'm retiring. I'll go in for a week or so to clear up the calendar, but I'm giving notice now."

"The accident?"

"Partially. I've lost the will for it, I guess."

"Your decision have anything to do with Katy, or Ardis?"

The judge's hands fluttered like wings across his robe. I stared out the window. The rain was now a steady barrage, a gray wall of water. My heart was like a hammer banging rapidly against my chest. I didn't want to be here. "Tell me about Swann."

The judge's expression didn't change. He held my eyes. "Swann?"

"He's on your court calendar. He's been there before.

He works as a line handler for the cruise ships where you got Patrick a job."

Just bowed his head, his eyes closed as if he were praying.

"This all connects back to Katy, doesn't it?"

Just raised his head. "You know who her father is?"

I nodded. "Brendan Scott."

"How did you learn that?"

"Joe Delgado told me."

The judge fell silent a moment. "And Swann?"

"Was the punk who stole the chalice Katy sent me. He'd been tailing me ever since I went to work for Scott and Delgado. I thought they'd put him on me in case that chalice turned up. Which is what happened. But they didn't hire him. Someone else did."

"Who?"

"Probably someone who knew Swann had a record. I was hoping you might have some ideas."

"Sorry, Bud, I can't help you."

"Did you know that Webb had been moonlighting?" The judge shook his head.

"He was working for Scott. Keeping tabs on me. And anyone else Scott needed some leverage against."

"Why?"

"Webb needed the money. He'd work for anyone who would pay him. And it didn't have to be on the level."

"I'm sorry to hear that." Just looked betrayed.

"That's between you and me."

Just nodded. "Why would he have been keeping tabs on you?"

"Scott thought I might turn up that chalice. I think he wanted to know about it if I did."

Just put his hands together, pressing his fingertips to his forehead. "Webb was working regular hours at the courthouse. How could he keep track of you?"

"He'd call me. I'd meet him for lunch once in a while."

"That doesn't sound too intrusive."

I nodded. Or rewarding, I thought. It was hard, too, for me to believe that Webb was able to get anything on me that would have been useful to Scott. There was, of course, the chalice, but Delgado had seemed as surprised as anyone that it had ever been in my possession. And I had another idea on that matter.

The rain eased up for a minute, then came down with renewed vengeance.

"I talked to Ardis last night. She came down to the club where I was playing. She'd had a lot to drink. She seemed upset."

"I'm sorry."

"You knew her husband, didn't you?"

"Only slightly." Just raised one eyebrow.

"What did you make of him?"

Smiling, Just shrugged. "Somewhat full of himself, but harmless enough."

"You knew he was involved in the salvage industry?"

Just shook his head. "I met him maybe twice several years ago. I don't remember that we talked about that."

"But you and Ardis talked about it."

"She mentioned it."

"She tell you that Jack had been suing one of the salvage companies at the time of his death?"

Just nodded.

"And that she had refiled that suit."

"I knew about it."

"Surely you more than knew about it. Didn't you advise her? Didn't she ask for your legal opinion?"

"I couldn't represent her. Tim Kelly's her attorney, Bud."

"I know that, but you could still have been an influence."

Just frowned. "I don't see how. Not from a legal position anyway."

"Of course not. But Ardis didn't have any money. She's got a house that's probably mortgaged to the hilt. Her husband had spent all his money dabbling for buried treasure. He left her with not much more than a house and a lawsuit."

"Poor judgment maybe, but that's not a crime."

"For someone like Ardis it may have been just as bad."

"What are you getting at, Bud?"

"It was an embarrassment. Ardis craves respectability. Too often that goes hand in hand with money. Maybe she needed one to get the other, even if it meant marrying into it."

"Bud, you're going too far—"

"Don't tell me you haven't thought about it. If you discovered it for yourself, that would explain why you retreated. Ardis came to me before your accident and tried to make light of your depression. She said it was natural for a man to get cold feet before he got married, especially one who had been alone as long as you have. Now I think she was just nervous, afraid that you'd learned something about her and perhaps had confided in me. I must have set her mind at rest."

"If that's the way you want it, Bud."

"What I want is the truth. How desperate was she, Just? Desperate enough to use you to get her hands on that chalice?"

The judge turned away, staring out the window, a nerve twitching in his jaw. Perhaps he was wishing, as I was, that the rain could somehow wash us clean. "How could I have done that, Bud?"

"Swann."

"You think I hired him?"

"It may be far-fetched but I have to examine the possibility. Ardis was listening at the door the day you came home from the hospital and we talked in here. I told you about the chalice then."

"You're right, Bud. Ardis is ambitious. I knew it, thought I could live with it."

"And she thought she could change you."

"And maybe she could have."

"What changed your mind?"

"She knew about the chalice. She'd talked about it. Her husband, Jack, had seen it when it first came up. It left an impression."

"Several impressions."

"But there isn't any connection between Ardis and Swann. At least not that I know about. Ardis knew nothing of my court calendar. And if your theory is right, she would be the last person to involve herself with someone like Swann." The judge's eyes flashed. "Ardis didn't have anything to do with the theft of that chalice, Bud. So drop it."

I nodded. "Thanks."

"What for?"

"I needed to hear you say that. To defend her."

"She's a good woman, Bud. With some faults, just like the rest of us, but she's a good woman."

"I'm sure she is. But I had to press the issue. You understand?"

Just grunted.

"Besides, I think I may know who was responsible for the theft."

"You want to share it with me?"

I stood up and walked to the desk. "Let me use your phone."

46

◇

The secretary for the shipping agent that handled the cruise ship dockings said that Swann was no longer employed with them. I told her that I was his parole officer and that he hadn't appeared for his regular weekly appointment. She gave me his last known address and phone number.

I called Swann's number. There was no answer. Then I called a cab. The rain was still falling steadily.

"You're sure you know what you're doing?" the judge asked.

"I'm sure."

"Be careful, Bud."

I had my raincoat on and was waiting on the front porch when the cab pulled up. I made a dash across the lawn and jumped in the back, giving the driver Swann's address, which turned out to be a two-story apartment block off South Street.

I recognized the place as one of the few remaining run-down establishments that catered to transients in Key West: cinder-block construction with a flat roof, paint peeling, a narrow lawn with a clothesline and plastic toys strewn around. In the parking lot the Buick would have been right at home with the other outdated cars. One of which, an old rusty Ford, sat with its hood up while someone tinkered with the engine. Swann. I asked the cabbie to park nearby, then I sat back and watched Swann work.

He was clearly frustrated by his efforts to get the car started. After five minutes of tinkering and trying to get the engine to turn over, Swann threw a wrench on the ground and walked back into one of the apartments. I gave the driver a twenty and told him to wait.

Swann's unit faced the courtyard and had one shuttered window beside the door. No one was around. By standing along the off-window side of the door I didn't think I could be seen if he was looking out. I listened but heard nothing. I knocked. Footsteps approached on the other side of the door.

He opened the door cautiously. When he saw my face, his expression changed like summer weather. He started to close the door. Jamming my foot in the threshold, I shouldered my way inside. "Take it easy, Swann, this is just a social call."

He backed into the room, shaken. I used my foot to push the door closed. We stood in a small, barren living room. A couple of packed bags were sitting in the middle of the floor. A toolbox was on a table and Swann was backing toward it. I sprang at him, grabbing one skinny arm as he tried with his free hand to reach the ball peen hammer that lay on the top of the toolbox. I jerked his arm, pulling him off center, then forced the arm behind his back.

"Shit, you're gonna break my fuckin' arm, man."

"That's right, Swann. That's exactly what I'm going to do. And after I break that one, I'll break the other one. Then I'll start on your legs." With my other hand gripping his scrawny neck I added some more pressure to his arm. He moaned and began to collapse to his knees. I forced him back up. He moaned again.

"There's only one way you're going to walk out of here without being crippled for life, and that's by talking." I pressured the arm again. "Do I make myself clear?"

"Yeah, man," Swann whimpered. "Take it easy."

I forced him in front of me while I surveyed the apartment. There was a tiny kitchen with dirty dishes stacked in the sink, a filthy bathroom opposite that. No bedroom. The couch was pulled out into a bed with soiled and tangled sheets. I pushed Swann down onto the bed, putting my knee in the middle of his back while I ripped the thin, dirty sheets in strips and used them to tie his hands behind him.

"Now, let's talk. It looks like you're moving. Where you going?"

"Getting out of this town, man," Swann said sullenly. "I can't make it here."

I shook my head and tapped him in the face with the flat of my hand with just enough force to bring some color to his cheek. "That wouldn't be smart now, would it? You've got a court date with Judge Watson next week. You miss that and you're in violation of parole. Then you've got a warrant out for your arrest."

Swann wriggled against the sheet binding his arms. I slapped the other side of his face. "Now where you going?"

"North, man. New Hampshire."

I grinned. "You look like a New Hampshire kind of kid."

Swann didn't say anything, just lay back awkwardly

against the couch, breathing deeply and staring at the floor.

"How would you like to have an attempted-murder charge filed against you before you go?"

That got his attention. "What the fuck are you talking about?"

"Did I stutter? I'm sorry. I'm talking about murder, Swann. The kind that gets you some heavy prison time."

"You're out of your mind. I never killed no one."

I stood up. "I believe you, but how about I open one of those bags? What do you think I'm gonna find in there besides a few pair of smelly socks?"

Swann didn't say anything. He didn't have to, his eyes spoke for him. I walked over to the bags, kicked them both, reached down and unzipped them, then squatted, keeping my eyes on Swann as I ran my hands through the bags. I found what I wanted on the bottom of one, wrapped in a T-shirt. I grinned.

"Now what would a New Hampshire punk like you be doing with something like this?" I held up the chalice.

Swann cowered down on the bed. "You know where I got it," he whined.

I walked over to the bed and took hold of one of his ears, twisting it. "I know where you got it. And you could have killed me getting it."

A bead of sweat appeared along Swann's hairline. "Make it easy on yourself. You take the rap for breaking and entering, or you bite the big one." I gave a gentle tug to his earlobe, then released it. "Now talk. Who set you up?"

Swann took a deep breath, his eyes cast downward. "A guy called me and told me to heist your place and what I was looking for. I was supposed to deliver it to him."

"What guy?"

"I don't know. He didn't tell me his name."

"Where were you going to deliver it?"

"A hotel."

"COD? How much?"

"Five hundred bucks."

"Once you saw it you decided you could fence it for more than that, right?"

Swann shook his head. "The guy knew about my record. He was going to get it straightened out."

"So why didn't you deliver?"

"I got to the hotel and the police were around and I overheard someone say that a guy had been punched out in the parking lot. I got scared and split. I waited for him to make contact, but nobody called me so I decided to boogie."

I nodded. Of course nobody called because the nobody had bought it, as Swann said, in the parking lot that night right after apologizing to me. For what he'd done. And was about to do. Webb, old buddy.

So that's how it had been. Swann had been working for Webb, and Webb had been working for Scott, supposedly keeping tabs on me. But he couldn't do it all on his own, not and keep up with his day job. So he must have hired Swann to do his dirty work, probably without thinking too much about it, not expecting it really to come to anything. It wouldn't have mattered to Webb that the punk was totally inept. All the kid had to do was watch and report back to Webb, who could then relay information along to Scott, or Delgado, and it would look as if Webb were doing his job. A chain of two-bit spies and snitches.

I looked down at Swann, who must have seen something ugly in my face, because he cringed, expecting another slap. That Swann had a police record, with an upcoming court date, meant that Webb wouldn't have had to worry about keeping him in line. Everything must have been hunky-dory until the punk reported to Webb that I'd gotten a package in the mail. Webb must have had some idea of what it was. He must have decided right then and there not to tell Scott, but to get it for himself, or at least check it out. If it was the chalice, then Webb knew that he had a shot at some real money, for the first time in his life. Too bad I was in the way.

Never trust a drunk was the lesson, especially not a drunk who's deep in debt.

I placed the chalice carefully on the floor and hauled Swann up from the bed. Then I grabbed another sheet and forced him into the bathroom. "All right, here's how it's going to go down. You never saw that thing in your life. You don't know anything about it. Nobody ever hired you to pinch it. You got that, Swann? I'm doing you a favor."

I shoved him down on the bathroom floor and used the other bedsheet to tie him to the water pipes running to the sink. Then I stood over him. "You're going to jail for B and E, but I'm not going to press charges. We'll see what we can do about getting the case you've got before Judge Watson dropped. Then you're going to boogie. Back to New Hampshire, or wherever. I just don't want to see your face around here again. Read me?"

Swann looked at me with what might have been gratitude or just stupefaction. He slowly nodded his head.

"Have a nice life," I said.

I went out of the bathroom, picked up the chalice, and tucked it inside my raincoat before opening the door. Brendan Scott stood there, water running down his face, a gun pointing at my belly.

◇

Going somewhere, detective?"

"Out for some fresh air. I got the feeling though that I may have to leave Key West to find it."

"Sooner than you think. Let's go inside and make ourselves comfortable."

I backed into the apartment. Scott came in and closed the door. "I see what you mean. This place isn't exactly home sweet home." Scott walked around, keeping the gun pointed at me while he poked around the apartment, pausing at the bathroom doorway. "Well, look-it what we have here. Nice work, detective. You want to introduce us."

"That's the punk I was telling you about who was dogging my footsteps. His name's Swann."

"I'll be damned. You thought I'd hired him? He doesn't even shave yet."

"I know now you didn't hire him. Someone else we both know did."

"And who might that be?" Scott remained propped in the doorway, giving Swann and me his divided attention. He seemed amused somehow by Swann.

"Webb Conners."

"Webb?" The amusement disappeared.

"That's right. I asked Webb to dig up some background on you and Delgado. You asked him to follow me. Turns out he double-crossed us both."

"Is that how this got here?" Scott tapped the chalice with the tip of his gun.

I clutched it tighter, as if there might be some safety in it. "The punk stole it from me."

"Stole it from you, huh?" Scott looked down at the terrified kid huddled on the bathroom floor, then back at me. "And just how did it come to be yours?"

"Katy." It took a moment for the name to get out of my mouth. "Katy Morgan sent it to me."

Scott snorted. "The whore?"

"Yeah, you could put it that way. Your daughter, the dead whore."

Scott's gun, which had been dividing its time between Swann and me, slammed into my abdomen so hard that I gasped. "Save it for family therapy, asshole. Now you want to connect the dots for me?"

"She wanted me to have it—keep it for her, I guess. She didn't tell me how she'd gotten it, but she was worried about losing it. Look, she didn't tell me a lot. I was on my way to see her the day she died."

"Let me get this straight. Swann here stole that cup from you and delivered it to Webb, right?"

"That was the idea. Except when Swann got to the hotel to make his delivery, Webb was gone already, dead. Swann must have realized it was worth something and decided to hold on to it. He waited a couple of days, then decided the best thing to do was to beat it out of town."

"Enter the shamus who'd figured it all out, and here we are. So why don't you take off your coat and relieve yourself of the burden you're carrying. Or maybe you were on your way to the boat to deliver it to me now."

I held the chalice up in the light of the single overhead bulb, turning it so the emeralds glinted. "Look at it, Brendan. Katy wanted to know her father and what she got was this. Maybe it meant something to her—a gift, sort of, from the father she'd never had. Or maybe if she'd kept it, she would have sold it and used the money to go to school, do something with her life with a little help from Dad."

"How was I supposed to know she was my daughter?" Scott's mouth twitched at the corner, but not enough to make it look as if he were in any kind of pain. "Her mother was a goddamn whore, too."

"But you did know. That's what makes this whole thing stink like a week-old cadaver. You knew who Katy was. You've known for a long time. But *she* didn't know that. Katy could live with the fact that she'd found her father. Maybe she could even live with the relationship that she had with him, but not when she realized you'd known, known all along, and you'd continued sleeping with her anyway. Did you tell her yourself? Or did Delgado? She found out Saturday night. She was out with both of you that night. One of you told her. Who was it?"

"Delgado." The gun wavered for a moment while the man behind it shifted his weight from one foot to the other. "They got in an argument and he told her. What's it to you?"

I shook my head in disbelief. "You're trash, Scott, the kind of scum that belongs under a rock. When she found out the truth, that you knew who she was all along, and continued having sex with her, it killed her. You might as well have turned the gas on in that trailer yourself. It was because of the knowledge she had that she couldn't bear the humiliation. If she'd had a stronger sense of herself, she might have hated you enough to try and kill you. A pity she didn't."

"You self-righteous prick. Who nominated you to judge me? Just give me the goddamn cup."

It seemed to me at that moment it wasn't the chalice I was holding, but Katy. "If you want it, you're going to have to come and take it. Or you can walk out this door right now and there's not a damned thing I can do about it, and nothing the law can do about it. I don't like that. What you did was wrong. Way beyond wrong. The word is *evil*. Katy trusted me to get to the bottom of this, to see that you were exposed, because she couldn't do it herself. She was too humiliated. So I've got to do it for her." I twisted the chalice a little and took a step back. "How bad do you want it, Scott? Bad enough to kill for it?"

"You talk too goddamn much." Scott raised the gun. "You think I won't kill you?"

"Go ahead." I grinned. "They'll send you to the chair, where you belong." I took another step toward the door. Scott's finger was on the trigger. "Kill me and you've got to kill the punk. You can't leave any witnesses, Bren. That's a double homicide. Premeditated. Too bad they won't be able to fry you twice." Another step back and I was in reach of the doorknob.

"I swear to God I'll kill you. Don't force my hand."

I stood there grinning like an idiot, a bead of sweat tickling my scalp. I had to clutch the chalice close to my body to keep my hand from shaking. With my free hand I was slowly reaching for the doorknob when the door suddenly flew open, banging into me and knocking me to the floor. Two shots exploded. I heard one of them thud into the wall between the door and the window casing in back of where I'd been standing. I could see where the other shot went. Brendan Scott lay on his back in a pool of blood.

I eased up onto one knee, reached out, and pulled the door open wider. Bill Eberhardt was crouched in the threshold, holding a gun at his side. A sickish smile played over his face when he saw me. My heart was thumping in my chest. "Where'd you come from?"

"Judge Watson called and told me where you'd gone. I thought I might get some answers to a few questions."

"Did you?"

"I heard enough. I've just got one question."

"What's that?"

"Were you really going to let him take a shot at you?"

I tried to smile, feeling the blood begin to circulate back to my brain. "I hadn't really made up my mind."

Eberhardt shook his head and stood up. We both walked over and examined Scott. He was dead. I went into the bathroom and untied Swann. Bill was on his cellular phone. After hanging up, he put the cuffs on Swann and started to take him out to the car.

"What do we do with this?" Eberhardt stopped at the open door and picked up the chalice I'd dropped.

"As far as I'm concerned, you can throw it back in the ocean where it belongs," I said, and followed them out into the rain.

48

A week later the judge and Ardis were married. I played at their small reception afterward. The judge was decked out in a tropical suit and a flowery tie that Ardis had given him. With his silvery hair and ruddy complexion he was the picture of health.

Over the top of the piano, I watched with some amusement as the judge dipped a triangle of bread into some hummus Ardis had prepared, along with other hors d'oeuvres, then responded to someone's toast, lifting his glass of champagne.

Patrick, who had served as best man, floated around the room, looking uncomfortable in his rented suit. The judge stopped him, putting his hand on Patrick's shoulder, and spoke to him quietly. Patrick smiled; they touched glasses, and Patrick drifted off. The judge came over to the piano.

"I feel good," Just said, "like this was the right thing to do."

"You look happy. I'm glad to see that."

Until today, we had spoken only once since I had left his study to pay my visit to Swann. I had wanted to know why the judge had called Eberhardt.

"Intuition," Just told me. "That kid was bad news. Too erratic. I've seen his type in court too many years now. You never know what they're going to do."

What the judge did, in the matter of the people versus Swann, and one of his last cases before retiring, was to give him a minimal sentence. I wasn't willing to press charges against him, wanting only to see him gone, back in New Hampshire.

On another matter, the judge had told me that after talking it over at length with Ardis, they'd decided to go ahead with wedding plans.

"What changed your mind?" I asked.

"You did. I had some uncertainty about Ardis, some of the same concerns that you raised with me the other day. I'm glad to find that I was wrong. That we were both wrong."

"I'm sorry if I had to be a little rough when I questioned you the other day."

"There's nothing to be sorry about. You did us a favor, Ardis and me. We're both grateful."

Now, standing across the piano from me, the judge smiled. "Take care of yourself, Bud. Ardis and I are going to travel a bit, get out of this burg more. She thinks it will do me good, and I'm inclined to agree with her. I'm actually looking forward to it."

I nodded. Someone came by and took the judge aside. I was content to remain the anonymous player. Many of the people here I didn't know, much like the night of the party Ardis and Just had thrown a couple of weeks ago. But there were others, familiar faces from the courthouse, most of whom managed to stop by to greet me briefly.

One of them was my ex-wife Peggy, who tried to keep a conversation going while I played. That was Peggy.

Finally, she said what I knew she was going to say. "I'm so sorry Webb couldn't have been here."

"A pity," I mumbled.

"Judy's still terribly broken up."

I nodded.

"We've both spent a lot of time reminiscing about the past. And of course that included you, Bud. You and Webb were such good friends, and we did have a lot of fun."

"It's something to think about," I replied, changing chords.

"If he'd only gone on a diet," Peggy mused. "Did you ever find out what was bothering him?"

"No, it must just have been a little episode, nothing to worry about. Webb was crazy about Judy."

Peggy nodded and sighed. "I know. He'd spent so much money though that Judy can't account for. At least he had a good insurance policy. That along with his pension. Judy's going to be fine."

"I'm glad."

Peggy smiled, seemed about to say something else, then leaned down and kissed my cheek before moving on as I watched Ardis make her way toward the piano.

She was in a beige pantsuit, trim and elegant. "I've never apologized for my behavior that night I came to hear you play."

"None needed."

"And of course I've never properly thanked you, either."

"For what?"

"Oh, so many things. Patrick for one. He's really taken to this treasure hunting. He's gotten a job with another outfit."

"I hope with good results." Leaving unspoken his father's efforts.

"And also for getting Just and me back together. I don't know what you said to him and in fact can't remember what you and I talked about that night—which is probably just as well."

"Nothing. Really nothing. It looks like you've worked some changes on the judge already."

Ardis laid her hand on my shoulder. "I hope for the better."

"I'm sure."

"Anyway, Gideon, here's to you." She lifted her champagne glass. I picked up my club soda from the top of the piano and we clinked glasses. "We're leaving the day after tomorrow for Cartagena."

"Bon voyage."

As Ardis glided away from the piano, I segued into "Love for Sale." She paused a second, then turned and winked at me. I winked back.